# DARK POWER

---

CHARLI CROSS SERIES: BOOK THREE

MARY STONE
DONNA BERDEL

❀ Created with Vellum

# DESCRIPTION

**Knowledge is power. But power can be deadly.**

Practical and fact-driven, Detective Charli Cross never imagined she'd hear the word voodoo in connection with a police investigation. That was before a body is discovered on top of a grave while a zombie-like man wanders the same cemetery...and they're both holding voodoo dolls.

What do a shady drug dealer and a retired bus driver have in common, and why does someone want them dead? Is voodoo's dark power at work, or something even more sinister?

Charli and her partner Matthew are determined to uncover the truth. But it's one step forward and two steps back as they delve deeper into the case and search for the legendary but elusive voodoo priestess who might hold the key to the mystery.

When the dark magic is turned on Charli, though, it's about to get personal...and deadly.

***Eerie and macabre, Dark Power is the third book in the Charli Cross Series from bestselling author Mary Stone that will make you fear the dark...and the light.***

*This book is dedicated to those who struggle with addiction and to the ones who love them.*

# 1

Heavy breaths echoed off the dark red brick of the alleyway as Jefferson Brown ran as fast as his arthritic legs would carry him. His own exhalations were all he could hear, drowning out any other noise, including any footfalls behind him.

Was he still being followed?

He desperately wanted to glance back, but there was no time to look around and double check. If he could calm his breathing, he might be able to hear what was happening behind him, but that remained an impossibility.

He'd been running for too long. His body was reaching a breaking point. If he didn't gulp air in heaving gasps, he wouldn't absorb enough oxygen to sustain himself. Hell, even sucking in oxygen like a fish out of water wouldn't help for much longer. But Jefferson was only a few blocks from home. It wouldn't be too far now.

Though he wasn't sure reaching home would change anything.

Dammit, why hadn't he just left well enough alone? Why

did he have to push, have to test the limitations of this world? Jefferson wasn't a believer. He never had been.

Even as a child, while his classmates would share stories of Santa or the tooth fairy, he shrugged them off as ridiculous. Jefferson was a man grounded in this world, the real world, unable to imagine anything he couldn't see with his own two eyes.

He had seen it now. In fact, it was right in front of him, smothering him, threatening to swallow him whole. He couldn't deny it, no matter how desperately he wanted to.

His friends had told him not to mess with a voodoo priestess. And he hadn't listened. Because what was there to worry about? What could a woman wielding voodoo possibly do if voodoo itself was imaginary nonsense? It was easy to feel invincible to her magic when Jefferson knew the magic wasn't real to begin with.

What a fool he'd been. This never had to happen. He could be home right now, carefree, his mind far from the realm of paranormal phenomena. If only he could go back in time, make another decision, refuse to ever enter into her world.

A world that consumed him now. She'd infiltrated his mind, blurred even his deepest memories. Every moment was an enigma, including this one.

*Why was he running? Why was he so racked with fear?*

Jefferson hadn't a clue who was chasing him, but the feeling that they were there to cause him harm was overwhelming. This fear ran deeper than any he'd ever known.

Danger wasn't foreign to Jefferson. Before this, he'd considered himself to be abnormally courageous, unable to be shaken. The way every muscle in his body trembled, that was no longer true.

When he arrived at the curve in the L-shaped alleyway, he nearly sank to his knees and sobbed. The streetlights at the end of the road were his saving grace. Jefferson was nearly home, his apartment only one street over. If he could just make it to his door, he would be safe.

The yellow streetlamps brought warmth into his body. Reminiscent of his childhood nightlight, they signaled to him the same thing his nightlight had...safety. In just ten feet, he'd be out of the darkness, onto the public street that led to his home.

The soles of Jefferson's shoes pounded the pavement more vigorously than a moment ago. With the hope that the streetlamps provided, he'd gotten a second wind. The increased speed caused the heavy glass in his pocket to thump against his chest, likely causing a deep purple welt. But Jefferson couldn't care less about a bruise. That was the least of his problems. It wouldn't be long now until—

"Jefferson."

A voice stopped him dead in his tracks. He knew that voice, though it had been a decade since he'd heard it. Was it really her?

"Mom?" The word was barely audible over the beating of his heart.

It couldn't be. In the back of his mind, with the tiny piece of his brain that was still holding onto the logical framework of reality, he knew it was impossible for his mother to call out to him.

She was dead.

He'd seen it himself. Curled up in her sterile, white hospital room, she'd taken her last agonizing breath as he held her hand.

This had to be a trick, more mind manipulation from the voodoo priestess. Unless...unless maybe it wasn't a trick at all. Perhaps the priestess had opened up a portal between the world of the living and the dead.

The idea would've sounded ludicrous a week ago, but

Jefferson's entire worldview had shifted in the past few days. If the priestess had been capable of all the evil she'd instilled upon Jefferson, wouldn't it be possible that her voodoo was capable of bringing dead spirits back to this Earth?

With each passing second, Jefferson became further convinced that he could sense his mother's soul nearby. Her voice came to him again.

"Jefferson."

"Mama!" His voice rang out in a way it hadn't since his childhood.

If he just walked back down the alleyway, he'd see her. He just knew it. His mother would hold him in her arms once more. She would kiss his cheek, and all the agony the priestess had put upon him would melt away, just like when she used to scare away the monsters in his closet.

"Jefferson."

He waltzed back into the shadows, dancing along the brick wall, as he reminisced on his childhood memories of her. This ordeal with the priestess would all be worth it if he got to see his mother once more. He only had to turn that corner, and she'd be standing there, her hazel eyes staring at him. Jefferson could almost see her figure, almost…

He wasn't wrong. As he rounded the corner, there was indeed a figure there. But it wasn't his mother. A menacing shadow loomed ahead.

Jefferson swallowed hard, working up enough saliva to enable him to speak. "Who are you?"

There was no immediate answer. In his scrambled mind, Jefferson couldn't identify the shadowy individual, but they were definitely familiar.

More shadows appeared on the brick walls, forming a line behind the person in front of him.

"Where's my mother?" Jefferson's hands trembled. The

cold night air swirled around him, causing him to shake even more.

The figure tossed its head back, an eerie laugh snaking its way into Jefferson's soul. Other shadow people mimicked the hollow, sinister sound. Inhuman noises filled the alleyway, growing louder as they bounced off the surrounding stone. So loud, in fact, that Jefferson clapped his chilled hands over his ears.

"Stop! Stop it!" Jefferson squeezed his eyes shut, somehow hoping that would help drown out the sound.

The ghoulish laughs only grew louder. It was as if the noise wasn't emanating from the outside but bouncing around inside his brain. The more he pushed on his ears, the worse it became.

Jefferson opened his eyes, only to find the shadow figures were closer now. He gasped, forcing his lids closed again.

"No, no, don't do this! Please, just leave me alone! I want my mama! Ma!"

With their footfalls came an icy wind, and despite his closed eyes, Jefferson knew they were approaching swiftly.

"Open your eyes, Jefferson." The voice of his mother was clear in his ears again, unmuffled by his clenched fists. This time, it was apparent his mother wasn't really here. But the comfort of her voice commanded him to obey.

When he did, the shadows were a mere foot from his face. Their demon faces were clearer now. Empty black eyes stared down at him, with smiles that spanned from one ear to the other. Razor-sharp teeth gleamed behind each pair of dripping red lips.

When Jefferson tried to speak, fear crept up his spine, his tongue drying out like a flower in the desert sun. Trembling hands moved to his mouth, but it didn't help words to form.

It wouldn't have mattered because, before his heart could squeeze out another beat, the demons descended.

# 2

Voodoo?

*What the hell?*

Detective Charlotte Cross still couldn't believe that her sergeant had seriously used such a word in connection to a police case.

Charli cleared her throat. "Excuse me?"

"I asked if either of you believe in voodoo."

It still didn't compute.

Charli glanced around her office, wondering if she was being punk'd. "Why?"

Sergeant Ruth Morris handed the official report to Charli and hooked a thumb in the direction of the door. "Get down to Bonaventure Cemetery and find out."

Two minutes later, she and her partner were in Charli's car and pulling from the Savannah Police Department parking lot.

"Hope you're ready for a ghost of a time." Detective Matthew Church peered at her from the passenger seat. Though he was clearly trying to be funny, a stiff smile was plastered on his face.

Seems like Ruth might have succeeded in scaring her partner. Charli rolled her eyes. "Halloween isn't for over a month, so it's a little early for ghosts."

"Oh, come on." Matthew tossed the report onto the dash. "You must think this is kind of spooky, right? Guy dies in the middle of a cemetery with a voodoo doll in his lap? It's giving me the creeps."

Charli was tempted to yell "Boo" just to enjoy his response, but didn't want her partner peeing on her little hybrid's interior. "No, I'm not bothered in the slightest. This is just another case in a sea of cases we've had lately."

Frankly, if she had to pick one that rattled her, it would be the one with the teenage girls turning up dead in horribly gruesome ways. Nothing in the paranormal realm could shake Charli, not when real life was filled with so much horror. What some sociopaths were capable of doing to their fellow humans, that was the real terror. But voodoo magic? Absolutely not.

"Don't tell me you believe voodoo is real?"

Matthew's shoulders rose and fell with a quick jerk. "I'm not saying that necessarily. But I can't say it's not real. There are things in this world we can't quickly explain with science and statistics, y'know?"

No, Charli didn't know.

Facts were the basis of her life while statistics helped guide her belief system. There was nothing she valued more than getting to the truth, and that wasn't limited to just her criminal cases.

But there was no point in arguing with Matthew about this now. She already knew she and her partner differed heavily on their approach to the world. He didn't use logic to ground him, choosing to rely on gut instincts and emotions to guide him through a case. His openness to the spiritual world seemed odd for a moment, but upon further reflection, it shouldn't have surprised her in the least.

Bonaventure Cemetery came into view, its bright green grass swaying softly in the morning breeze. Half of the grass was cut, the other half looking in need of a trim. The groundskeeper must have been in the middle of landscaping when he discovered the body.

A Savannah PD car sat next to the entry gate. "Do you know who's on scene already?" Charli pulled her car right beside it before parking.

Matthew cupped his brow, an attempt to shield his eyes from the bright morning light. Squinting, he nodded toward an officer in the distance. "Looks like Trigg to me."

Charli wasn't tall enough to see over the brick fence and couldn't confirm Matthew's observation until they made their way past the entrance and into the wet grass. Indeed, it was Officer Kenny Trigg, and he was scribbling in a notepad. As he wrote, he took small steps around the gravestones, jumping around like he was playing a slow-motion game of hopscotch.

Matthew shot Charli a concerned glance before catching the officer's attention. "You okay there, bud?"

Officer Trigg morphed into the very definition of relieved. His shoulders relaxed, and the hand that was holding his notebook drifted to his waist.

"You have no idea how glad I am to see you guys."

"What were you doing there? Walking all zigzagged, I mean." Charli used a finger to mimic the motion.

"Oh, uh, nothing. It's stupid. My grandma always told me it's bad luck to walk over a grave. I've been trying to stay between them, but they're so damn close together and..." Trigg averted his eyes.

"Cemeteries bother you, Officer?" Matthew grinned, wiping his sleeve across his forehead.

"More than you know." A gust of wind sent a couple of dead leaves skittering across the grass, and Trigg nearly jumped a foot. His face flamed in embarrassment. "I'd love to pass on the updated report and get the hell out of here."

*What was the deal with these guys? Freaked out over voodoo and cemeteries? They had a job to do.*

Shaking her head, Charli grabbed her own notepad out of her pocket and set about focusing on the new case. "What's going on?"

"Got the call over the broadband police channel that somebody had found a dead body in the cemetery. At first I thought, duh, where the hell else should a dead body be? But I guess this one was sitting above the grass, on *top* of one of the gravesites."

Yeah...that was a bit weird.

Charli waved a hand for the officer to continue. "Go on."

"I got here, and the guy is fully dressed, hair fixed, no blood, clutching some crazy looking doll in his hand." Trigg visibly shuddered. "Doll looks almost exactly like him. The guy could've been sleeping if it wasn't for the pale white skin."

Matthew stuffed his hands into his pockets and rocked back on his heels. "Do we know who it is?"

"I don't have a positive ID yet. We're working on it. Forensics is with him, taking some samples and photos. They'll collect skin cells from his nails and mouth, but they agree it doesn't look like there was any kind of struggle. Might be a medical incident, sudden cardiac arrest, or something?" Trigg's shoulders hitched up to his ears. "I dunno, being here in the daylight is already giving me a heart attack, so I can't imagine what it feels like at night."

"And he was definitely in the cemetery last night, not early this morning?" Charli glanced up from her notebook.

"Groundskeeper was here before morning light, so yeah,

it had to have happened last night. Come on, I'll take you to the body."

Trigg evidently wasn't bothering to hide how disturbed he was, seeming eager to escape the scene. As he turned around, Charli and Matthew smiled at each other, both finding it amusing that this case could frighten the officer this much. Trigg was a burly guy, standing at six foot two. If he had a beard and a plaid shirt, you could mistake him for a lumberjack. Not exactly the kind of man you'd expect to be frantically pacing in a cemetery.

When they reached the body, though, Charli understood why this case was so disconcerting. She wasn't as fearful as Trigg, but there was something bizarre about the victim's appearance.

His face had lost all color, but the corners of his mouth were almost smiling, as if he was enjoying a pleasant dream. His light blue button-down shirt was perfectly pressed and tucked into his khaki pants. The man was on his back in a supine position, hands folded on his stomach.

Charli's gaze was drawn to the doll. Badly sewn with uneven stitches, the doll shared the victim's jet-black hair and wore a similar outfit.

"What the hell?" Matthew sucked in a breath as he took it all in. "I've never seen anything like this. Our victims are usually doused in blood or crumpled up in a heap. He looks untouched, but there's no way in hell he got into this position himself. Someone had to have placed him like this."

He looked like a corpse minus the casket.

"Unless he decided to lie down like this prior to his death." Charli didn't think this likely but wanted to list all the possibilities. She peeled her gaze away from the still form to concentrate on the forensic pathologist and her assistant bookending the body. "You got any information for us?"

"Nothing much." Iris Ford shrugged and sat back on her

heels, sweat shining on her dark skin. "Liver temp suggests that death occurred eight to twelve hours ago. We'll know more once we get him on the table. I'm sure Soames will be giving you a call."

Charli almost smiled at the mention of Dr. Randal Soames. She liked the concise nature of the Georgia Bureau of Investigation's medical examiner very much.

She turned to Trigg. "You said the groundskeeper found him?"

"Cedric De Bassio. You'll have to go to the front office to find him. He says he won't be caught dead anywhere near..." Trigg waved a hand at the victim, his eyes drifting down to the deceased man once more. "I can't blame him."

The office was an old brick building that sat at the far-right end of the cemetery. It was likely erected at the same time as the cemetery back before 1910. Matthew put a hand on the gold knob attached to the chipping scarlet front door. The chime of a bell echoed once they stepped in.

Cedric's eyes opened at the sound of the bell. *Either we interrupted his prayer, or he was asleep.* Charli would have bet on the former.

"I'm sorry, but we're closed to visitors right now." Gray curls adorned the older man's head while crow's feet garnished the corners of his eyes.

"We're not visitors. I'm Detective Cross, and this is my partner, Detective Church. We're here to ask you about what happened this morning."

Cedric swallowed hard, his ping-pong-ball-sized Adam's apple moving up and down his scrawny throat. "Did they get that body out of here?"

"Not yet. Our forensics team is still taking a look." Matthew ran his hand along the smooth top of the cherry front desk.

Cedric gave a quick shake of his head. "He needs to be out, right now. Papa Legba lingers where his victim resides."

*What the hell?*

"Papa Legba?" She turned to Matthew, who seemed as confused as she felt.

He only shrugged in response.

"You don't know Papa Legba?" Cedric made the sign of a cross over his heart as a bead of sweat trickled down his temple. "The spirit in charge of deciding who can contact the spirit world? No priestess can enact her magic without the help of Papa Legba."

"You're familiar with voodoo culture?" Charli noted this, though she hardly thought Papa Legba was going to be a suspect in their investigation.

Cedric's almond-colored eyes grew dark. "Voodoo culture? It's not a culture, Detective. That implies it isn't real and only exists in the head of a few believers." He crossed himself again in what appeared to be an unconscious movement. "But voodoo is very real, I assure you. I've seen it done myself. Though I haven't seen any curses done this openly in Savannah for many decades."

Charli jotted this down too. She had no idea that voodoo had ever been openly practiced in Savannah. In fact, before this moment, Charli didn't know there were any places in the USA where voodoo was consistently practiced outside of New Orleans.

"Sir, may I ask how you came across the body?"

"I was tending to the lawn, as I'm ought to do every Monday morning. When I saw him, I thought it was some kinda prank."

Matthew lifted a finger. "Do you get pranked a lot?"

Cedric scowled, reaching to put a stray pen in the holder on the desk. "Damn kids around here don't know when to quit. They get me every damn Halloween with some practical joke. Figured they were getting their jollies off early this year. Thought the body was a fake at first, a..." He waved both hands in front of him, outlining the shape of a person.

"A mannequin?" At least that's what Charli hoped he meant.

"Yes. A mannequin or something. But when I saw it was a real person, I rushed over to help the man. Didn't take long to realize he wasn't breathin'. And the second I saw that doll in his hand..." The older man shuddered so hard Charli wouldn't have been surprised if his clothes flew off his body.

"What did you do next?"

He snorted at her question. "I rushed off to the office to call the police and told 'em I wasn't approaching that...that... thing anymore. I don't need Papa Legba and his minions infiltrating my life. I've worked this cemetery for thirty years and managed to never bring home an angry spirit. I wanna keep it that way."

Cedric was superstitious. That much was clear. "And you didn't see anyone else in the cemetery when you arrived this morning?"

"Nope. It was a nice, quiet morning until I ran into that body."

Charli flipped to the next page in her notebook. "You don't recognize the man? He never visited the cemetery?"

Cedric ran a finger along the top of a dusty picture frame, the photo inside appearing to be a younger version of himself, his arm draped around a smiling woman of about his same age. "No, I know all the regulars. We don't get too many visitors stopping by more than once, not when half the cemetery died a hundred years ago." He tapped his temple. "My mind is as sharp as when I was twenty years old. I'm confident I've never seen that man in my sixty-one years on this Earth. And I'm tellin' ya, something ain't right about him. That man messed with something bigger than himself."

Although Charli didn't believe in voodoo or ghosts, the way his hoarse voice croaked out the last sentence sent a chill down her spine. There was no denying the case was unsettling, even for a nonbeliever.

*Rinnnggg.*

Charli flinched in response to the classic ringtone of her partner's phone. The older man stared at Matthew, wide-eyed and curious.

Matthew grinned. "Relax, you guys never heard a phone ring?" He stepped away, but Charli could still make out his side of the conversation. "Detective Church speaking...yes, we're on scene now. We just...wait, what?"

Charli craned her head forward, expecting more information.

"Okay, yes, we'll go look right now." Matthew put his phone back in his pocket. "They got a call back at the precinct. Someone is walking around the cemetery. Apparently, the caller thought..." Matthew glanced at Cedric, as if considering whether he should say this within earshot of him.

But if it was happening at the cemetery, the groundskeeper would find out eventually, anyway. And Charli was damn eager to hear what was going on. "The caller thought what?"

"They thought he looked like a zombie."

The room went eerily still as they all processed this information. After a moment of heavy silence, Cedric crossed himself again. "I told you, something ain't right."

# 3

"You don't have to come with us if it's going to make you uncomfortable." Charli was concerned for Cedric, who was muttering under his breath.

"I'm responsible for this cemetery." The groundskeeper paced back and forth. "Not gonna stand around while some zombie goes digging up graves in search of brains."

Matthew snorted, throwing up both hands. "Oh, come on. He obviously isn't a zombie. You think you've got a voodoo curse and a zombie in this graveyard on the same day?"

Even though he appeared outwardly frustrated, Charli knew her partner well enough to see the edge of anxiety in his expression and body language.

In contrast, Cedric's anxiety was written all over his face. "Stranger things have happened."

Matthew rolled his eyes at his partner. "If you've got a stranger story than that, I'd like to hear it."

Officer Trigg was already on the parking lot side of the cemetery's fence line, following a man in an untucked navy t-shirt. At first, Charli could only glimpse the back of his head, but she made a mental note of every feature she could determine. Six-foot tall male with a scalp so shiny the sun beamed off his ebony head.

The closer they got, the clearer Trigg's shaky voice became. He kept a six-foot-wide berth between himself and the catatonic man.

"Sir, I need to know your name." Trigg's voice quivered. It was obvious the morning's events had him rattled. "If you don't comply, I'll have to place you under arrest pending further investigation. This is trespassing."

"Can't a man just come to work and mow the grass without a damn catastrophe happening?" Cedric's tone may have been frustrated, but his tense shoulders rose as his hands fidgeted in his pockets. Charli sensed his fear.

"Come on, man, just say something!" Trigg waved his hands in the air, attempting to get his attention.

"Oh, no, no, no." Cedric's mutterings forced Charli to turn around. There was no longer any façade of anger covering his terror. His eyes gleamed with pure, unadulterated horror. "That isn't normal!" Cedric pointed in the man's direction.

He had turned around now and was walking along the fence line in the other direction. One step appeared out of sync with the other, causing a wobbling gait. His legs did indeed resemble something from an episode of *The Walking Dead*.

That wasn't what was most disconcerting, though. Cedric was most likely panicking about the man's face. During her days as a beat cop, Charli had seen people slack-jawed from being high on opioids or benzodiazepines. She'd also seen individuals with eyes bulging out of their heads from crack cocaine or methamphetamine. But never had she seen someone with both at the same time.

Every inch of white in his eyes was visible. His jaw seemed almost unhinged from the rest of his face. And despite how wide his eyelids were held up, there was no life in his pupils.

"Relax, Cedric, he isn't really a zombie." Matthew gave the groundskeeper a pat on the shoulder, though even his voice was unsteady.

Charli snapped out of her own unease. Whatever was wrong with this man, there was a perfectly logical explanation for it. And since he wasn't attempting to bite any of their throats out, zombification simply wasn't one of them.

"Sir, can you hear me?" Charli lifted her chin and took several steps forward.

But she garnered no more of a reaction than Trigg had.

Trigg ran a hand through his hair as Charli moved even closer. "What the hell is wrong with him?"

"I don't know. Does he keep turning around and following this one stretch of fence?"

"Yes, for the last few minutes, at least. Should we cuff him?"

"No!" Matthew put up a firm hand. "Do not touch him. If this is drug related, physical contact could escalate the situation. Let's call in the paramedics so he can get whatever medical help he needs."

"Medical help?" Cedric threw up his hands. "You think this is drugs? I've lived in the slums of Savannah my whole life. I've seen my share of addicts. Drugs don't do this! And look at his damn hand!"

Charli had been so absorbed by the odd expression on their suspicious person's face that she didn't notice it at first. But sure enough, clutched in his grip was another cloth doll.

Matthew's jaw dropped as he took a step backward. "What the hell?"

"You call the paramedics." Charli raised her voice, hoping to snap Matthew back to reality. "I'll fill Ruth in. Trigg, you stay with him."

Trigg's displeasure was evident when he bit his lip, but no protests were forthcoming. He was bothered, but he wouldn't shy away from doing his job.

Charli dialed her boss. "Sergeant Morris speaking."

"It's Cross. I'm out at the cemetery. We've come across something new you should know about."

Ruth wasn't pleased to learn that not only was there another incident at the cemetery but that, for whatever reason, they both were found with voodoo dolls in hand. She wanted information that Charli didn't yet have and could only promise to find as soon as possible.

By the time she disconnected the call, the ambulance had already arrived.

One medic, a woman with short, jet-black hair, walked up behind Charli. "What's going on here?"

Charli motioned to the zombified man. "We'd love to know ourselves. This man is unresponsive verbally, walking around in a fugue state. He moves back and forth along the fence but doesn't answer anyone. No clear injuries, but something isn't right."

"Hmm." The medic placed her hand under her chin. "It's almost like he's sleepwalking, huh?"

*That's unlikely.* How often did sleepwalkers make their way out of the house and down the sidewalk? The nearest residential neighborhood was blocks away. He would've had to cross multiple streets to get here. He could be homeless, but most of the unhoused citizens of Savannah congregated closer to the downtown area. There weren't many resources out here, no stores or bathrooms nearby.

The medic and her partner, a stout male in his early twenties, began to approach the man, their steps cautious.

"Sir, we'd love to get you some help." The female used a soft, calming voice. "Can you tell us your name?"

*Silence.*

Her partner reached for the hand with the voodoo doll. "That's interesting. Can I see that?"

The response was immediate. This was the first moment the man acknowledged anyone else's presence. Not verbally —he remained quiet—but he jerked his hand back when the paramedic attempted to touch the doll. His grip tightened, causing his knuckles to turn white.

The paramedic's hand fell back to his side. "Uh, okay, well, you can keep that. But can you come with us?"

The medics had a hell of a time trying to get him into the back of the ambulance. They ended up herding him like a cattle dog darting for a stray sheep. The whole time, they kept their feet near the back of his so he couldn't twist around and walk back along the fence line. The male medic stayed in the back with him while his partner hopped into the driver's seat and turned on the lights and sirens.

"I swear, this isn't normal." Cedric's words hung in the air as he made his way back to his office.

Charli couldn't disagree with that. She didn't believe either of these cases was related to voodoo or zombies, but she had no other obvious explanation for the strange behavior. It wasn't normal, not like any other case she'd ever experienced before.

She didn't know whether to be excited or terrified.

# 4

"Who the hell is this Papa Legba?" Charli took a sip of her coffee, savoring its warmth as the vehicle's AC blasted in her face.

Matthew sipped his own drink next to her. They'd decided they wouldn't follow the ambulance right away. It would take time for the paramedics to admit the man and the hospital staff to run tests, so they grabbed coffee and now sat in the hospital parking lot, recounting details of the case.

Matthew reached to turn the volume down. Somehow, he'd convinced Charli to let him listen to country music in her car, which wasn't her favorite genre. She was glad when the twanging faded away to almost nothing. "You know, I do remember the Papa Legba thing, now that you mention it."

Charli set her cup down in the holder. "Really? I've never heard of it."

Matthew nodded. "My dad was into that kind of thing. I remember when I was young, he used to read to me from a book called *In the Garden of Good and Evil*. I don't know if he really believed it, or he just liked to get me spooked before bed. I used to look forward to him reading to me every night, regardless of what book it was. Wow, that was a long time ago."

Charli was tired of all the voodoo talk but found herself wanting to know a little bit more. "Remember much from the book?"

"No, not really. But I do remember that voodoo magic is often not done alone but in conjunction with spirits from another realm. Papa Legba was one of them. People had to make offerings to him, things like tobacco, candy, and alcohol. What's really disturbing is he used to require sacrifices of babies in order to conduct some of his darkest magic. Something about them being innocent souls."

How could people really believe this stuff? "That is positively deranged."

"Well, not all voodoo is. It isn't always black magic."

Charli chuckled before sipping more of her coffee. "You say that like you actually believe some of that magic is real."

Matthew adjusted the AC vent, turning it until it blew directly on him. "You have to admit, today was damn weird. I mean, one guy is dead with a voodoo doll, and the other is walking around like he's got a craving for brains. That is beyond strange."

"We're going to walk in there and be told that he's on some new street drug that causes him to behave that way. You watch." Charli would not allow herself to be sucked into paranormal discussions. It wasn't relevant to the case, not really.

"And those dolls? The fact that they both had one?"

Charli let out a long breath. "I don't know. Maybe it's a new toy they're selling nearby. You know, a booth at the farmers market or something, where you can get a doll that looks just like you."

Matthew shuddered and reached for his coffee, tilting it to get the last gulp from the cup. "I don't know about you, but I would never buy a doll like that, especially not if it resembled me."

Charli didn't wish to entertain this any longer. "Let's head inside, see if they have any information for us."

It was early on a Monday morning, a rather slow time for the emergency department. When Matthew and Charli made it to the front desk, the medical staff had already taken John Doe back and begun a series of tests.

"Did he speak to you?" Charli addressed the emergency department nurse responsible for his care.

The woman's honey-colored hair was pulled back in a tight bun. "No, and we've been unable to figure out who he is. But have a seat out here. The doctor will grab you when we know something."

Matthew and Charli sat in two chairs pushed against the ER hallway.

"I really hope something turns up in the tox screen. If we show up to the precinct empty-handed, Ruth is going to have a cow." Charli pushed her hair off her forehead. Her pixie cut was beginning to grow out. She should probably schedule a hair appointment soon, but her work schedule hadn't been particularly forgiving lately.

Matthew leaned back in his chair and pulled out his phone. "Ruth wasn't too happy to hear about another voodoo incident at the cemetery, huh?"

"Not in the slightest."

The doctor appeared twenty minutes later, but not with the answers Charli was hoping for.

"Well, I certainly suspect he's under the influence of some kind of drug. His tests all came back clear, including the MRI that ruled out any head trauma. But whatever he ingested, it's not coming back on our usual tox screen. We'll have to test for more obscure drugs."

Matthew pushed to his feet. "But you're sure drugs are involved?"

The doctor pulled off a pair of examination gloves, tossing them in a nearby trash can. "There doesn't appear to be anything physically wrong with him, and his liver enzymes are elevated, suggesting drug consumption, yes. I suppose there is still the possibility that his current state is related to his mental health, but if it's drug related, we will see his head clear up within the next twelve hours. In the meantime, you aren't going to get much out of him now. We can call you when he's responsive."

"Thank you." Charli reached into her jacket to pull out her card. "We'll be in touch."

"Well, that's not news Ruth is going to be happy about." Matthew kicked a small pebble in the gravel as they made their way to the parking lot.

No, she wouldn't be, and Charli wasn't in the mood to be verbally filleted right now. "Maybe we don't need to head back to the precinct yet. In a couple hours, the drugs might run out of his system, and then we could go back to Ruth with real news."

"Sure, but what are we going to do in the meantime?" Matthew kicked a stone out of the way. "If we tell Ruth we were just screwing around and grabbing lunch instead of returning to the precinct, she's going to find that equally annoying as us coming back empty-handed."

He wasn't wrong. If they were going to procrastinate, it had to be related to the case. And that wouldn't be easy, considering the only piece of evidence they had was a pair of matching voodoo dolls.

Charli came to an abrupt halt just feet from the car. "Wait, you said your dad used to read to you from a book about voodoo, right? The one you were telling me about earlier."

Matthew slid his hands into his pockets. "Yeah, he did. But what does that have to do with our case?"

Charli put a hand on her hip, ignoring her partner's question. "Do you think the book is still popular today? Popular enough that they might have it at the public library?"

"I'm not sure. I mean, it's possible." Surprise shot his eyebrows up to his hairline. "Do you want to read it? I didn't think you had any interest in learning about voodoo."

"I don't. But maybe it's the kind of research that will keep us out of the precinct for a couple hours."

Matthew chuckled to himself. "I like the way you think, Charli. And I'm proud of you for branching out. Voodoo books are a lot different from the typical serial killer biographies you normally read."

Charli rolled her eyes and decided to keep her smart comment to herself.

Reading didn't seem like a bad way to spend an afternoon. Charli didn't have to believe in voodoo to enjoy reading a few books about it. And while voodoo magic hadn't killed the man in the cemetery, it was certainly related to his death. Perhaps he was a follower himself, or if there was foul play, maybe the person who had killed him believed in it. Regardless, the more background information Charli had, the greater insight she'd have into the minds of those involved with this man's death.

Charli hadn't been to the Carnegie Library since middle school. The ceilings seemed lower than back then, the walls narrower. But it was still a gorgeous library. White columns sat on either side of the rows of bookshelves. Four large, rectangle windows adorned the walls nearest to the help desk. Behind the cherry desk sat an older woman, her gray and purple streaked hair cascading down to her shoulders in waves.

"Excuse me, could you help me find a book I used to read?" Matthew stepped in front of Charli. The movement wasn't a rude one. On the contrary, Charli appreciated that Matthew was quick to volunteer in social interactions such as this.

"What's the name, dear?" The librarian's long purple nails started clacking against her keyboard.

"*In the Garden of Good and Evil.* I can't remember who the author is."

The woman tucked a strand of hair behind her ear and continued to peck at the keys. "Not a problem. We've got it right here. It'll be in the Foreign Religion section. Make a right over that way. Are you interested in voodoo history?"

Matthew glanced at Charli. "You could say that."

The woman's smile exploded with excitement. "In that case, you must do your research on Tany Speers. She's a Savannah native, you know."

Charli stepped closer to the desk. "I'm sorry, Tany Speers?"

The librarian's eyes brightened. "You're interested in voodoo but never heard of Tany Speers?" She was one of those people who spoke with their hands, and her layers of bangled bracelets clanked every time she moved. "She's a local priestess, or so they say. I don't know anyone who's ever actually tracked her down. You could say she has an almost mythical presence here in Savannah."

Perhaps voodoo culture was a lot more prominent here than Charli had initially thought. If even this sweet old librarian was aware of voodoo legend, how had Charli never heard of it?

"Thank you. We will certainly keep her in mind."

Matthew flashed his usual charming smile before heading toward the Foreign Religion aisle.

"Was everyone but me taught about voodoo during their childhood?" Charli wasn't sure whether to be worried or thankful.

Matthew shrugged as he ran his hands over several book spines. "Come to think of it, I feel like a lot of my school friends knew about these legends too. All right, here it is." Matthew pulled the book out with two fingers, almost like he was afraid the thing might bite.

Charli had expected a black cover with images of sinister looking dolls adorning the cover. Instead, it was a deep emerald green with sketches of different faces, though none of them were particularly creepy.

Charli raised her eyebrows, giving her partner a pointed look. "I thought you said your dad used to scare you with this. It looks like a regular book to me."

"It is, in a lot of ways. I told you, not all voodoo is creepy, black magic. But a few legends did bother me. Like..." Matthew started flipping through the pages until he made an abrupt stop. "Okay, here it is. Papa Legba."

Charli stepped closer to get a better look. "Wait, him? That nice looking old man? You made him sound so much worse than he looks."

"He looks nice, sure. But he's basically a," he glanced around and lowered his voice, "god of the underworld. It's only through him that someone can speak between those two realms or, if you're really brave, walk through them."

Charli shivered. *Did people actually believe this nonsense?* "Wait, so someone can go to the underworld?"

"Sure, but you might not come back. Technically, we're all going there one day, right?" Matthew flashed a cheeky smile.

Charli was about to shoot back a sarcastic reply when her phone rang.

"Damn, it's Ruth." She let out a long sigh before bracing herself to answer. "Detective Cross speaking."

"So much for avoiding a media hellstorm." Each word entered Charli's ear like a knife. "When were you planning to tell me that your zombified cemetery man had been caught on camera?"

Well, that couldn't be good.

# 5

Neither Charli nor Matthew had seen anyone filming at the cemetery. It had been only them, Trigg, and the groundskeeper. None of them had their phones out at any time.

But when Matthew and Charli reached the precinct, everyone was watching the videos. They'd already spread on the majority of social media channels. If a local news agency wasn't working on the story already, they soon would be.

Ruth met the detectives in the lobby. "Would it have been so hard to make sure nobody was filming near you guys?"

"Nobody was. Here, can I see that?" Charli waved down a nearby beat cop who was walking by. He had the video open on his phone, his eyes glued to the screen in shock.

"Sure." He handed her the phone, continuing to watch the video over Charli's shoulder.

Whoever had made the TikTok added an eerie music track to the background. Admittedly, the music combined with the dead expression on the zombie man's face was pretty spooky. But it was an embellishment of the real situation.

"Look, you can see in this video that he's still outside of the cemetery gate." Charli tilted the phone to Ruth. "We didn't even know about our dead body yet. Kind of hard to keep anyone from filming before we're aware of the situation. And they certainly made the situation out to be a lot more dramatic than it really was." Charli handed back the phone to the cop, who scurried off. Nobody wanted to be around when Ruth was about to explode.

No explosion was forthcoming, though. Ruth was a reasonable woman. She could see as easily as Charli that this situation couldn't have been avoided. Still, she raised two fingers to the sides of her head to rub her temples.

"Please tell me you have some news. This is going to spiral quickly. I want to have answers for the public."

"Answers for the public?" Matthew threw up his hands. "It's just a guy drugged out of his mind wandering the city. He wasn't violent. He didn't attack anyone. He wasn't even talking, for crying out loud. Why does the public need an explanation?"

Ruth's eyes narrowed. "Because whether we like it or not, this video will disturb people. The man may have been harmless, but he doesn't look like your conventional drug addict. Ever since the stories of zombie men eating the faces off people in Florida a few years back, it's easy for people to get spooked at this kind of behavior."

Ruth was right. Logic didn't determine what scared the citizens of Savannah. The media did. And it was almost a guarantee they'd take this clip and run with it, especially with Halloween on the horizon.

Ruth stood up straighter. "You said he was drugged out of his mind. Have we confirmed that?"

"Not with any specific drug." Matthew wilted a bit as Ruth rose, and Charli suspected it was because he knew they had no real information yet. "The doctor is going to run more tests and call us when he's coherent. Right now, we still don't have an ID or know what he took."

The sergeant put her hands on her hips. "Fantastic, so we have virtually no information to provide for media inquiries."

Charli considered mentioning their research at the library so that Ruth would at least know they were trying to find answers. But in retrospect, it seemed a little silly. How was reading childhood books going to help them with this case? It was all a bunch of legends.

"What about the dead man? Have you identified him yet?" Ruth pinned Charli with one of her signature no-nonsense expressions.

"Not yet." Charli slid her hands into her pockets. "But forensics is working him over now. They'll run his prints."

"Excuse me, Sergeant?" Detective Janice Piper's voice came from behind Charli, sounding a lot meeker than usual.

Ruth let out a huff of air. "I don't like the sound of that already."

The slim redhead gave Ruth an apologetic look. "I'm sorry, but it looks like one of the local news channels has already posted an article about the zombie…er, man…at the cemetery."

"Oh, for crying out loud! It's been five hours!" Ruth smacked a hand to her forehead. "At least they don't know about the deceased individual. When they find out, this story will take off like a rocket."

"Uh, about that…" Janice bit her lip.

"Don't tell me they wrote about him too."

"No, they didn't. But they did notice the voodoo doll in the hospitalized man's hand, so the whole thing has a horror spin to it. The story is already getting a lot of attention."

Charli and Matthew exchanged quick glances. They

didn't need to speak to communicate with each other. The concern they shared was written all over their faces.

"Fantastic! We've got a horror movie investigation on our hands." Ruth pinned the detectives with her gaze. "You guys need to get on top of this and fast. If you don't, I may just call up my aunt. She practices voodoo too, you know. Everyone in this precinct is getting a curse if we don't get a handle on this."

Matthew's eyes widened. "Wait, seriously?"

"Am I seriously going to curse the entire precinct? No, obviously I will not, Detective Church." Ruth shook her head and strode down the hallway to her office.

Charli didn't think that was what Matthew meant, though. She was curious about the same thing. *Did her aunt actually practice voodoo?* Once again, Charli felt as though she was the only one not privy to this mysterious religion.

"What can we do? It's not like we have information to go off. We don't even know the victims' names." Matthew eyed Charli, hoping for answers.

She was on the verge of responding when Janice Piper hopped in front of her instead. "You could always go through past cases for any voodoo-related activity. This might not be the only voodoo crime in Savannah."

"That's a perfect idea." Matthew patted Janice on the shoulder, and she practically purred with contentment.

It was a decent idea, but Charli had been about to suggest it herself before Janice nearly toppled her over trying to get Matthew's attention. Even worse, Matthew never seemed to notice that Janice was vying for affection from him. He also didn't acknowledge how Janice had it out for Charli.

Charli wasn't fooled, though. Janice's attention toward Matthew had increased ever since his divorce. That made it more than a little obvious what Janice's intentions were. Thankfully, Charli didn't think Matthew shared that interest.

Charli shuddered to think what a nightmare Janice would become if she and Matthew were actually dating. She'd likely be the overly jealous type, ready to pounce on Charli for so much as touching Matthew's desk.

"Perfect, let's go do that." Charli sidestepped Janice, who deflated when Matthew began to walk down the hall with his partner.

Charli couldn't concern herself with Janice's nonsense right now, though. Ruth wanted answers. Her aunt didn't have to curse the entire precinct. Ruth's frustrations would serve as curse enough.

# 6

"Well, this is the last one." Charli groaned as she scrolled through the case file. "And it happened nearly two decades ago. This is going nowhere."

There were only a few cases with any reference to voodoo, and they were all out of date. Not to mention, none of them had any references to dolls. Mostly, they were clear-cut cases of users on hallucinogens claiming to have seen some spirit or conducted a spell. None of them had any relation to the case at hand.

"I can't believe we still haven't gotten any positive identification." Charli tapped at her warm computer desk. The sun was streaming in, heating the surface of the wood.

Charli waited for Matthew's answer, but one didn't come. She swiveled around in her chair to find him glued to his computer screen. Had he found some case she hadn't?

Without another word, Charli got out of her seat and walked around to his desk. But he wasn't looking at past cases.

"Seriously? You're browsing the web?"

Matthew laughed. "Browsing the web? Whatever you say,

Grandma. And no. Actually, I'm using google-fu to research our case."

Charli slid herself onto his desk next to the computer, allowing her feet to dangle off the side. "Google-fu? Is that an official detective tactic?"

Matthew flashed Charli a sly grin. "It is, actually. And it's helping. Ever heard of a drug called scopolamine?"

Charli scrolled through her pharmaceutical knowledge, which didn't last long. "I'm not sure."

"It's also known as Devil's Breath. It's pretty common in South America, apparently. Comes from Columbia but is often used in dangerous areas in Brazil to commit crime. Ring any bells?"

Charli narrowed her eyes, wondering if this was a trick question. Using drugs was obviously a crime in and of itself. But how could a drug be utilized for further crime?

Then it hit her, and Charli snapped her fingers, remembering reading something about that. "Didn't some gang use something like that in Paris to rob people?"

Matthew pressed his finger to the tip of his nose. "Yep. Supposedly, it makes victims behave like zombies. You can convince other people to commit a crime for you, and all you need to do is blow a little of the drug into your victim's face."

"That sounds a little too convenient." It would fit the profile of their zombie victim, but was a drug really capable of that?

Matthew began clicking away on his computer. "I'll send you the link. Read about it for yourself."

Charli returned to her desk to pull up the email. The computer whirred like an airplane engine readying for take-off. While the outdated desktop struggled to load the website, Charli rested her cheek in her palm and sighed.

When it finally loaded, she skimmed the small black text. It did indeed contain accounts of supposed scopolamine victims who claimed they'd committed crimes under the drug's influence. But this still seemed like an easy excuse to avoid accountability. She went ahead and started her own google-fu search.

"It's a dead end." Charli ran her cursor over a drug website article. "Says here that evidence of scopolamine causing victims to act as zombies is entirely unfounded. They've never been able to prove this side effect. It might make people more amenable to suggestion, but it doesn't turn them into zombies."

"Okay, well, what about this?" Matthew waved Charli back over to his monitor. "Have you ever heard of *The Serpent and the Rainbow?*"

"Is this another voodoo story?" Charli tilted his computer screen toward her. "Because, no, you already know I don't have any knowledge in that area."

"Not a story, but a novel. It was published by a former Harvard scientist. He was doing research down in Haiti and was told the story. Evidently, a group of voodoo priestesses were taking the venom from puffer fish and giving it to individuals to make them appear dead."

Charli tried to make the pieces fit in her head but couldn't. "Why would they ever want to make someone appear dead?"

"To make themselves look more powerful, I guess. They wanted to convince people they could raise the dead. So they'd administer the drug, and even doctors would confirm a patient's death. Then they'd do their spells, and the victim would return to life."

Charli rolled her eyes, leaning forward on the desk. "Is that even true?"

"It is, apparently, though the story isn't taken very seriously because they made a horror movie out of it with the same name. Still, this Harvard scientist witnessed it and published the case study."

Charli hopped off the desk. "That's all very interesting, but it isn't providing us with any answers. I don't think you're doing research for the case as much as fulfilling some of your curiosities."

From the beginning, Charli could tell this case was personally interesting to Matthew. He obviously was familiar with voodoo from his childhood, and she couldn't blame him for wanting to know more. But she'd point it out if he was going to drive them off track.

"What?" Matthew's eyes narrowed in defense. "Of course, this is relevant. This voodoo practice inspired the entire genre of zombie stories." He tapped the folder of information they'd gathered so far, which was slim. "And then we find a living zombie with a voodoo doll in his hand at the cemetery? Seems relevant to me."

That was a bit of a stretch. "Slow down there, cowboy. First of all, 'living zombie' is an oxymoron. And second, that man is nothing like the puffer fish case. He didn't appear dead. He was walking about just fine."

Matthew leaned back in his chair. "But he did seem drugged."

"No, he appeared to *be* on drugs. But there's no reason to think someone else drugged him. We know plenty of people in Savannah take drugs of their own volition."

Matthew shrugged. "Sure, but are they ever carrying voodoo dolls around of their own volition?"

What could she say to that?

Charli wouldn't try to deny how strange of a situation this all was. And the double voodoo dolls definitely lent to the theory that these two men were both victims of the same person. But Charli wouldn't allow her view to narrow on this case. She was open to all possibilities.

But Matthew had given her an idea. "Whether he took the drugs willingly or not, we know the drug didn't show up on a normal screening, right?"

"Right." Matthew raised an eyebrow, clearly not quite following Charli's train of thought.

"And he had that voodoo doll in his hand. We know from your google-fu that puffer fish venom is drug-specific to voodoo culture. What if there are more drugs utilized in voodoo culture?"

A smile lit up Matthew's face. "You're absolutely right. I wonder if we can find research on the subject? Surely there are specialists we can find who would be able to guide us."

"Maybe someone who studies the biochemistry of exotic animals? I mean, if the puffer fish is any indication, it seems that voodoo followers used natural drug extractions in their spells." Charli didn't know where to find a biochemist with such a specific background. "On second thought, maybe we should start with vice. If voodoo is this prominent in Savannah, surely they've run into some of these obscure drugs."

Perhaps if they forged ahead with their own research, they'd be able to call back to the hospital and suggest drugs to test for. At this point, Charli would do anything to keep this case moving. The faster they sped along, the happier Ruth would be.

And the sooner she'd never need to hear the word "voodoo" again.

Hopefully.

# 7

A deep breath filled my lungs with a bouquet of floral scents as I lowered my face over the glass teapot where a once red rosebud had turned sickly pale. The whiter it became, the more crimson the water turned.

Lifting my face toward the ceiling of my home, I smiled, reminded of the times I had visited my gran's home as a child. I felt safe here, just as I felt safe in my gran's home all those years ago. The sun shone through a window to cast lines on the floor beneath me, warming me even more.

Slowly, I began to dance between those lines, picking up speed as I clapped my hands together. The songs of my homeland rang out from inside my soul, and I smiled, serenity filling my being. As I danced, a wave of nausea overcame me, and my hands began to tremble.

Reaching for the back of a chair to steady myself, I stopped dancing, willing the nausea to pass. I would not let it get in the way of my ritual.

It was only from the bellowing of my native tongue that I could access my power. I took a deep breath as the nausea subsided a little, gripping the cloth and straw figures in my hand to the point of pain, causing scratches to form against my palm. Blood trickled down my wrist, but I didn't care because I would spill my blood freely to help my curse.

I was wise, strong, and full of vitality that most would never know. At least I used to be. Now...? I didn't want to think about that. I only wanted to think of all I could achieve in the present and near future.

A priestess in my magic, a queen in my community, I wouldn't let my brothers and sisters fall any longer, wouldn't hesitate to end anyone who tried to stop me.

A heaviness covered my soul, and I released a lingering sigh. I didn't want to end the enforcers, not really, and I would avoid doing so if they could be spared, but there was no length I wouldn't go to in order to protect my mission.

The enforcers just needed to behave, and thankfully, I had the power to make that happen. With this spell, I could guide them away from my direction, and as long as they were compliant, I wouldn't have to take things any further.

After finishing my dance, moving more slowly now to save my strength, I set the two dolls reverently on the floor before me. Having already ground down my herbs in my mortar and pestle, I poured them into the rose water before selecting the doll with the pixie haircut. She was shorter in stature than the doll of her partner, and I had given her a round face to match her oval cheeks. They were rough images of the nosy detectives, but that didn't matter. Dolls didn't have to be exact. They only had to be set with the right intention.

And I had my intention.

I would stop these two from discovering my true nature. Of course, I would allow them to continue their search because, after all, if I commanded them to cease their investigation immediately, it would only raise more flags.

I had to allow them to believe they were moving forward

on their case without ever discovering me. They simply could not discover me. At least, not yet.

With all my strength, I dunked both their heads in rose water at the same time and chanted to Baron Kriminel, the Saint of all Criminals. I knew he would share my hatred of these detectives since, in his life, he had been sentenced to death for his criminal activities.

A thunder roared through my body, and I felt it rise from the dolls and into my shoulders. Yes, my wishes would be granted, and those pesky detectives would no longer be an issue, allowing me to continue my good work.

And if I couldn't, darker spells would wipe them from this Earth. I wouldn't relish having to do it, but now that I had offered guidance to their souls, it would be their own fault if they resisted me.

# 8

Before settling on detective work, Charli had considered a career as a vice cop. That career choice often entailed a great deal of undercover work, which was a task Charli found intensely interesting. Ultimately, Charli knew herself well enough to know that would never work. She was a horrible actress. It wouldn't take much to throw her. She'd never been able to feign friendship with anyone she didn't like. How was she supposed to do it with criminals?

"Hey, Officer Lancaster, can we pick your brain?" Matthew waved down the first cop he could find in the vice department.

"Detective Church, Detective Cross, good to see you. Sure, I've got some time." He had a bottle of soda in hand, likely out of the vending machine in the lobby. He twisted the cap and started sipping as Charli and Matthew broke down their case.

"I'm sure you've seen the video of the zombie man walking around Savannah. You know, the one with the voodoo doll in his hand?" Matthew made a gripping motion with one hand, shuffling his feet and staring straight ahead.

Officer Lancaster chuckled and rolled his eyes. "Oh, yeah, I've seen it. Don't envy you two for having to deal with it. I heard Ruth is livid. Can't say I remember any doll, though."

"Well, I assure you, there was one." Charli heaved out her trusty notepad. "He's not our only case right now that seems tied to voodoo. We thought maybe you or someone else on your team may have come in contact with any groups dabbling in the dark magic. The doctor suspects our guy was drugged, but nothing showed up on a conventional tox screen."

The officer took a long drink from his soda before twisting the cap back on. "Ah, yeah, it wouldn't. We've had a few Haitian drug busts. Can't say that most of them are too different from our usual hits. A lot of LSD, mushrooms, ayahuasca, primarily hallucinogens. But in some cases, we'd find an odd assortment of ground up herbs, most of which were difficult to identify. One guy on the black market was selling toad genitalia. Evidently, it contains a bufotoxin that puts people right in a comatose state."

Charli jotted everything down. "A bufotoxin, huh? And what about some of those herbs? Did your team ever get any of them identified?"

"A couple, yeah. I can only think of one off the top of my head. Curare. It stood out because it had such a weird background. Like the toad bufotoxin, it knocks people out of their minds. Very rare in the USA, it comes from a plant called Strychnos toxifera. We did use it briefly in the 1940s as an anesthetic, but it didn't take long for it to be discontinued for medical use."

"If it's rare and discontinued in the U.S., how do people get it?" Matthew massaged the back of his neck, glancing at his partner's meticulous notes.

Officer Lancaster opened his soda again and took another drink. The bottle was already half empty. "It's rare here, but not uncommon in South America. Still used by shamans to this day for medical procedures. Most of it is smuggled in at the border."

"Interesting." Charli only glanced up a few times as her pen darted across the page.

The officer raised a finger in the air. "You know, I'm sure I'm forgetting a few herbs. I've got a guy on my team who went undercover with a Haitian gang. I'm sure he remembers a lot more than I do. I can have him contact you guys with what he knows."

Satisfied she'd gotten all the details, Charli slammed her notepad shut. "That would be amazing. Thank you. We really appreciate all your help. This case has been a doozy."

Charli wasn't feeling too bad about their progress, actually. They'd only been assigned the case this morning, and despite not yet knowing the name of their victim or the type of drug they were dealing with, they'd made headway.

The chime of Charli's ringtone echoed from her pocket. She pulled it out and directed her attention toward Matthew. "It's the hospital. Let's step out into the hall."

Once they reached a place where nobody else was milling around, Charli answered on speakerphone. "Detective Cross here."

"Hello, Detective. It's Dr. Wu calling."

"Dr. Wu, hello." Charli shot Matthew a hopeful glance and crossed her fingers. "Have you been able to identify any drugs in our John Doe's system?"

"Afraid not, but he's not John Doe anymore. He's starting to come back to himself, only barely, but enough to tell us his name is Carl Perkins. I wouldn't run right in to question him or anything. He's still very out of it, but perhaps in a few hours."

"Carl Perkins, got it." Charli nodded at Matthew, signaling to him that he should write the name down. "And we may have a list of possible drugs to test him for. I have a colleague curating a list for me right now. Though you could start with something called curare as well as any other bufotoxin you're familiar with."

"That is supremely helpful, thank you." The doctor sighed, sounding weary. "I don't know if it's because he's still under the influence and doesn't remember, but Carl is swearing he didn't take anything. We've been pulling teeth to get answers to no avail."

Charli tried not to read too much into that. Like Dr. Wu had said, perhaps Carl didn't yet remember what he'd consumed. But him being drugged against his will added a new dimension to this case. "Please call us with any more updates."

"I certainly will."

Charli pocketed her cell. "We've got a name. That's definitely a place to start."

Matthew nodded, a slow smile spreading over his face. "Let's see if Carl Perkins has a record of any kind. And while we're at it, it wouldn't hurt to look for any cases where curare or bufotoxins were involved." He held out a fist for Charli to bump.

She did, adding a little explosion of fingers at the end. "Sounds good to me."

# 9

On the walk back to their office, there was a short silence between Charli and Matthew. Not an uncomfortable silence, never that. They knew each other well enough to allow the other to sit with their thoughts.

Though, at the moment, there wasn't much to think about. They'd only started to scratch the surface of their case.

"Any plans for this weekend?"

She wondered if Matthew was tired of thinking about voodoo and magic. Maybe he needed a moment of normalcy before they jumped right back into focusing on their case.

Charli ran both hands through her hair, her lips fluttering with an exhale of exasperation. She didn't do small talk well, especially when it was focused on her. "At this rate, my weekend plans will be this case. And probably yours too, so if you had plans, I'd cancel them."

Charli couldn't pretend this bothered her. If it wasn't for the case, what would she do? Read her crime novels at home and order in Chinese food? This case would surely be more interesting than that.

The smile lines around Matthew's mouth deepened, and

he shook his head. "Oh, come on, Charli. You have to learn to live a little. Go out with friends sometimes. Hell, go on a date. You're telling me you never ended up going out with that GBI joker?"

"GBI joker?" Charli didn't know why she was playing dumb. She couldn't lie to Matthew. He knew her too well.

"Yeah, Preston Powell."

Did Matthew know that Preston had asked her out the last time they ran into each other? He couldn't have overheard. He was too far down the hall by the time Preston had asked. Perhaps he was just assuming based on the slight flirtations the agent had been sending her way. Or maybe he had picked the first single decent-looking male who had come to his mind.

"Even if I wanted to see Powell, I don't have the time. You should know better than anyone what this job does to your social calendar."

Charli hoped that response wouldn't make it too obvious that Preston had indeed asked her out.

It was intended to be a light tease, but Matthew's face fell flat. "Yeah, so I can tell you, you don't want this job to eat your social life alive. Don't end up in your thirties divorced, living in a crappy one-bedroom apartment, with a daughter who only texts back when she feels like it."

Charli bit her lip. She was never good in situations like these, when she had to offer unsolicited comfort. And what was there to say? The divorce had obviously been hard on him, and no words from Charli were going to improve the situation. She decided the best move was to continue to try to keep things light.

"To get divorced, I'd have to actually get married. And to get married, I'd have to see someone outside the precinct. Since that will never happen, I'm probably in the clear."

Matthew let out a long, slow sigh. "The point of my story

was not 'never get married,' Charli. Don't end up lonely, so put yourself out there. Date. Even if it is with an annoying geeb, it's a start."

Charli wouldn't say it aloud, but she was already considering that. The nights got lonely, and she grew tired of spending all her time by herself. But Matthew didn't need to know that Preston had suggested a date or that Charli was entertaining the idea. She didn't need to see Matthew turn into the protective big brother stereotype, as she knew he would.

Time for a big fat change of subject.

"All right, why don't you look up digital records on curare, and I'll see what I can find on Carl Perkins?" Charli pulled the office door open for both of them.

"I'm on it."

There wasn't much of a record on Carl Perkins. The only mark on his file was a court dispute over a late rent payment from fifteen years ago. From that, she was able to pull up his address and contact information.

Charli then used Matthew's favorite detective tactic: google-fu. Carl wasn't on any social media sites, but there was an article that referenced him. An obituary.

The death was of a Micah Perkins, Carl's son. The article identified Carl as a retired bus driver in Savannah's public school system. While there wasn't any information about how Micah died, Charli was curious whether they'd have any record of it in the system. If the death had required a 911 call, it would have been noted in the files.

Sure enough, Charli found information regarding Micah's death from four years ago. It was from acute intoxication by fentanyl, according to the coroner's report. Whether Micah had knowingly ingested the drug wasn't on the record, but Charli knew the most likely scenario was that it was accidental. The poor guy was only twenty-six when he died.

These days, numerous drugs were cut with fentanyl to increase their effect. Since the drug was one of the strongest opioids available, a dealer could multiply profits by mixing heroin with a small amount of fentanyl. The amount of product a dealer had to sell was minuscule when fentanyl was involved because such a small quantity of the drug was capable of producing such a potent high.

Unfortunately, fentanyl didn't just produce a more severe high. It was also much more deadly. And a regular heroin user could easily consume too much of the drug without realizing it was cut with fentanyl. If someone didn't administer Narcan promptly after such an event, death would occur in minutes.

"Find anything on Carl?" Matthew's voice jolted Charli in her chair after the twenty minutes of silence. "I haven't been able to find anything helpful on curare or other bufotoxins."

Charli leaned back and stretched, raising her arms over her head and clasping her hands together. "Yeah, a few things. No record, but he used to be a school bus driver, and his son died of a fentanyl overdose a few years ago."

"Tragic, but that doesn't give us much to go off of."

"No, not really."

Another voice penetrated their quiet office. "Perhaps I can help."

Ruth leaned on the doorframe, and Charli couldn't help but wonder how long she'd been standing like that. She really needed to do what her eye doctor suggested and look away from the screen every once in a while.

Matthew recovered first. "What do you got?" He pushed his chair back from his desk, his hands folded in his lap.

"We've got an ID on the deceased man in the cemetery. His shoes were custom-made at a nearby shop. We tracked him down through the label. He is Jefferson Brown, owner of the Rising Moon. I take it you both are familiar with it?"

They were. The Rising Moon was a shady tavern on the south side of the city. It was generally considered to be a hub of illicit activity. Drug deals, prostitution, the cops were called out there for fights on occasion. It wasn't exactly an upstanding Savannah establishment.

"We've been able to identify our zombie man as well." Matthew stood from his chair. "Well, the doctors were, anyway. He's Carl Perkins, a retired school bus driver."

Ruth chewed her lower lip. "A retired school bus driver and the owner of the sketchiest bar in town. Kind of an odd combination."

It was. Which was why Charli still wasn't sure the cases were tied together. But there were enough connections to explore it further.

"Find out if they knew each other or were related in any way." Ruth turned to leave.

"Will do." Charli called out down the hall to her boss, who gave her a thumbs-up and kept walking. Ruth didn't need to wait for further confirmation. She knew when she said something needed to be done, Matthew and Charli would make it happen.

Her phone rang again, and she hoped it was Dr. Wu calling to say Carl was ready for an interview. But it was from a number she didn't recognize.

"Detective Cross speaking."

"Cross, it's Lancaster. Just wanted to let you know I had my colleague email you a list of all the herbal supplements and illicit drugs he's run into with the Haitian gangs. Hope you find it helpful."

Charli was impressed. "Wow, that was quick. Thanks so much."

"No worries. I know how fast-moving your cases can be.

Wanted to do anything I could to help. If there's anything else I can assist you with, just let me know."

Charli paused. *Hmm, perhaps he could provide her with more insight.*

"Actually, I should ask, have you or your guys done any work with the Rising Moon?"

"Yeah. We've sent a few undercover cops that way. We suspect the owner is operating a pretty large drug ring, though we haven't been able to pin him down."

That was exactly the kind of news Charli was hoping for. "That owner you're talking about wouldn't happen to be Jefferson Brown, would it?"

"Yes. Why do you ask? Have you had issues with him?"

An image of the dead man flashed through Charli's mind. "You could say that. What do you know about him?"

"I know the Rising Moon has been in his family for decades, and it's been a drug den that entire time. It was well-known in the eighties for being an easy access point for coke and meth. I know Jefferson hasn't strayed far from the family business, but the man is a phantom. He keeps his tracks covered well. We know his hands are dirty but have never been able to catch him or any of his dealers. Our file on him is light, but I can send that your way as well."

"That would be fantastic."

"I'll get it sent over right away."

Matthew, who had been listening to the conversation, stood up from his chair to walk over to Charli. "So, Jefferson was a shady guy, presumably the kind of man someone would want to hurt."

"Probably safe to say someone did. I don't think he positioned his own body carefully, folded his arms across his chest, and then quietly died. The voodoo doll is likely a symbol, maybe from one of the Haitian gangs?" Charli launched a new internet window to conduct a new round of google-fu. They needed to find out who wanted Jefferson dead.

"But if the voodoo doll is a sign, why did we also find one in the hands of a retired bus driver? How could someone with a squeaky clean record be tied into whatever mess Jefferson Brown got himself into?"

Matthew made a good point, and there was only one way to find out. They needed to talk to Carl. Right now, he was the only one who would be able to explain if there was any connection between himself and Jefferson.

It would have to wait, though. And not only because Carl wasn't yet alert to his surroundings. Charli had received a text from the medical examiner, Dr. Randal Soames.

*We're ready when you are.*

# 10

Charli knew that Matthew wasn't a huge fan of stopping by the medical examiner's office. No matter how hard he tried to fight or deny it, going over a victim's autopsy results made him queasy.

Charli didn't share his soft stomach, though, and she and Soames had become close over the years. They had a good-natured friendship, and he was an expert in his field. He never failed to provide crucial information, which they needed right about now.

The examiner was waiting for them in the examination room with Jefferson's body. The odd smile was still plastered on the victim's face, which felt out of place with the long incision lining his torso.

"You guys handled that one quick." Charli stared down at Jefferson's rigid body.

Unlike most other corpses Charli had seen on the job, Jefferson could've been sleeping. Even here, at the medical examiner's office, it was as if he climbed onto one of the metal tables and drifted off for a nap.

Charli thought this would make it easier for Matthew to

stomach, but he was still tapping his fingers against his thigh.

Soames shifted his gaze between them both. "It wasn't easy, I'll tell you that. But your sergeant made sure we were expediting the case."

"Yeah, she is eager to get this one nailed down after that zombie footage hit the net."

*Hit the net?*

Charli was a little more self-conscious about her referrals to the internet after Matthew pointed out she sounded like a grandma. He wasn't wrong. Her internet slang was straight out of a late nineties sitcom.

"Haven't seen it, but I'll be sure to check it out after we finish, though." Soames turned around to collect his notes. "Cause of death is most certainly an intentional poisoning."

"Intentional?" Matthew kept his eyes set on either Soames or Charli, not straying to the body between them. "How could you know that it was intentional and not accidental?"

It was the same question Charli was asking herself. It seemed impossible for someone to know whether something was consumed intentionally from an autopsy.

"There is no way he could have ingested this accidentally. The plant doesn't grow in North America. Whether he consumed it himself or was poisoned by another person, the consumption was certainly intentional."

"What is it?" Charli had her hand on her phone, ready to pull up the list of drugs Officer Lancaster had sent her to cross-reference. But she didn't have to. She recognized this name right away.

"A drug called curare. It isn't common here. In fact, I've never run into it during a medical examination. Our initial tox screen didn't pick it up, so I had to pull out the big guns on this one. I've read about it before, but it was bizarre to see it in action. It doesn't perform like more common poisons."

"How so?" Charli loved to hear Soames extrapolate on his

wealth of knowledge. It was important to the case, of course, but even outside of that, she enjoyed learning about all the obscure information the examiner provided.

"Normally, in a poisoning, I see exterior signs. Ruptured blood vessels in the face, vomit, discoloration in the eyes. But there was nothing like that in this case. Externally, he appeared completely normal."

"Trust me, we noticed that on the scene." Matthew shuddered, swallowing hard. "Absolutely eerie."

Perhaps that was why Matthew still appeared so shaken, despite the lack of gore in Jefferson's death. In spite of appearing unharmed, the man was dead in front of them. When Charli considered this further, it was creepy.

And it brought up questions about what Jefferson's last moments must have been like. Did he experience the same fear Charli's other victims likely had in their final moments? Or was the peaceful expression on his face a sign he died without stress and had, in fact, simply drifted off to sleep?

She hoped for the latter.

"I'm sure it was worse to sec out in the field." Soames threw up a hand, gesturing around the room. "In here, dead bodies can never seem truly out of place."

Charli didn't want to get off track. "If there were no external signs, how exactly does this poison take its victims?"

"It's a paralytic, actually. Gradually, the victim will have a loss of movement. The neurotoxins will take over the brain first so that the victim can't even properly explain what is happening to them, if they even understand. Slowly but surely, their body will cease to move, and the lungs will follow. It's death by asphyxiation, but in the most drawn-out way."

Well, that answered her earlier question about whether Jefferson felt any fear. A pit formed in the bottom of Charli's stomach. That was a death so torturous she couldn't fathom it. Once, as a young child, her grandmother took her to the community pool. She was just learning how to swim and allowed herself to drift too far into the deep end.

In what had seemed like an instant, Charli had gone from happily breathing above the surface, to full-on panic as she searched for air. It was only a moment before the lifeguard swooped her up. Her grandma had been keeping a careful eye on her. But that one moment without oxygen was enough to instill a lifelong fear of asphyxiation.

It would be bad enough to die in a drowning scenario. Charli never imagined a situation where she'd feel herself suffocate slowly, her lungs increasingly growing heavier before they failed to receive any more oxygen.

Matthew must have been picturing the same scenario. "Holy crap, what a way to go."

The examiner let out a humorless chuckle. "It isn't pleasant, no. But, again, it is extremely rare in the U.S. In South America, they boil the bark of trees that contain the alkaloid. Historically, arrows and darts were dipped into the gel the bark creates and thrown at enemies."

"That's brutal." Matthew's voice was barely above a whisper.

"You seem pretty knowledgeable about this. Could you tell me if curare ever has more minor effects?" Charli fidgeted as she waited for the M.E.'s answer.

"How do you mean?"

"I mean, if given in lower doses, could it have a different impact? We have another man at the scene of this crime who didn't cease moving but had a very wobbly gait and couldn't speak to us."

The M.E. tugged off his gloves, folding one inside the other before tossing them in the trash. "Yes, at lower doses, it is nonlethal. That sounds in line with its effect. I'd get your guy tested."

"Already on it." There was a bit of pride in Charli's voice. She couldn't help it. It was nice to feel like they were actually ahead of a case for once.

Discovering the link between the two men and this drug made it clear their cases were connected. They still needed to wait for a tox screen on Carl Perkins, but that wouldn't take long.

And Charli was willing to bet both of these men had not drugged themselves with curare. It didn't seem like the kind of drug anyone would take recreationally.

The question was, if both men had been drugged, then by whom? Who had it out for both a shady drug dealer and a retired bus driver?

Charli was determined to find out.

# 11

"*We sure have had two strange cases pop up today, haven't we, Tom?"* The perky blonde anchor smiled through the television screen as if she was staring right into my eyes.

*"That's right, Miranda. You've probably seen the Savannah cemetery zombie video that has been circulating on social media. But what you likely haven't heard is that there was a bizarre death at the Bonaventure Cemetery. It occurred only hours before the zombie video was filmed."*

The way news anchors spoke pained me, annunciating every syllable, drawing out their sentences, leaving their viewers hanging on every word. Those poor, blind fools.

I couldn't shut off my small box television set, though, as much as I wanted to. I had to find out what they knew about Jefferson and Carl.

It was ludicrous that news anchors would just admit to the public where a police investigation was headed. Didn't they know whoever was responsible would be tracking the police movements closely?

But, as much as it saddened me, that was the world we lived in. They'd rather trade vital secrets for viewership, even if it meant putting police officers and other people at a disadvantage. Everything today was about getting noticed, about getting views, about attracting advertising money. The love of money being the root of all evil in this world didn't become a cliché without good reason.

Pain shot through my head, and I slowly massaged my temples. I drew in a deep breath, waiting for the pain to lessen. The next words from the news anchor got my attention.

*"The police believe these two cases may be related. The deceased individual, whose name has yet to be released to the public, was found holding a doll similar to the one the zombified man had in his grip."*

*"Sounds like Halloween came early this year, Tom."* The woman shivered delicately, though I thought it was more theatre than from real fear.

Irritating.

A man was dead, and this was what they did? They made flippant jokes about Halloween? This callousness was why I rarely turned on my TV. People's attitudes were an abomination. The "look at me" mindset was a large part of what was wrong with our society today. I ached for humanity.

With my mind lingering on the woes of society, I leaned into my drooping couch as the news shifted to the weather. The cushions were worn and faded with many decades of use, the arms tattered and bare in spots. I reached for my glass of water that sat at an end table, caressing multiple vials and crystals before I found it.

To some, my home may have had too much clutter, but it was sacred to me. Each surface held a number of my treasures that were invaluable, especially in my spells.

And it didn't much matter how jumbled my home was since I didn't let people inside, anyway. If I did, I'd have to explain the clutter.

I never got lonely because I coveted solitude, needed it to thrive. From my many years spent on this Earth, I had learned it was best to keep people at arm's length. That didn't mean I locked myself in my home, but rather, I locked everyone else out.

As much as it troubled my soul, there were few good people in this world, and even those who believed in their hearts they were doing the right thing would often cause undue harm. It was possible to have good intentions and be genuine but still be genuinely wrong.

Like those cops.

Soon, they'd be investigating Carl and Jefferson's cases and doing their best to find out who harmed them, but they shouldn't be seeking me out. They should be thanking me since I did them a favor. I had done everyone in this community a favor.

Although I knew I would never get any thanks, I was at peace with that. My form of justice would always be frowned upon because people saw voodoo as some evil, dark magic.

I chuckled at the misconception. Voodoo was an agent for good. Yes, it could be used with evil intentions, but so could anything else.

When a person got into a car accident and entered the hospital in horrendous pain, the doctor would give them strong narcotics to provide relief. The dealer on the corner could offer the same thing, but his intent would be to cause harm to the body in hopes of profiting off a new addiction. My thoughts drifted to my own conversation with a local doctor, but I forced his words out of my mind.

Since anything could be used and abused and nothing was inherently good or evil, I could only make sure my own goals were pure of heart. It was humans who turned to the dark, to greed and allowed themselves to be pulled into its depths.

And although my intentions were pure, I still struggled with what I had to do, with what I had already done. I had taken a life. I shuddered, the weight of what I had done a sobering realization. My actions would always cause me deep psychic harm. It was not easy to take from someone what the spirit world had given.

It had to be done, though. I knew I might have to pay for it at some point, but that was a sacrifice I was willing to make. If I knew my community would be safer, I was willing to do anything. Sure, I might not see eye to eye with many in the community, and I avoided other humans as much as possible, but I would do right by them. That was my burden.

*Rap rap rap.*

A heavy-handed knock to the metal frame of my screen door jolted me back to reality. It could only be one person. Most people were not brave enough to venture up to my door.

I scooted off the couch cushions, indented with my figure, and reached for my purse on the floor by the door. The cash I kept in there was nowhere to be found. Where had I put it? Since I had always been meticulous about where I kept my money and always knew exactly how much I had, this concerned me. I was too young to be this forgetful. I was too young for a lot of things, but here I was.

I glanced at the door. "Just a moment. I'll be right there."

Pinching the bridge of my nose, I willed myself to remember where I had put the cash. I looked in the brightly colored purse again, rummaging around through the pockets. Some worn bills caught my eye, and relief swept through me.

When I swung the door open, he was stoic, as usual. His dark skin shined against my porch light, his empty eyes staring at me unblinkingly while he reached into his pocket and pulled out a vial.

"Thank you. It's two hundred dollars, as usual."

He lifted his chin in an almost imperceptible nod, and I expected him to walk away in silence, as he often did.

"You know the cops are getting involved now, right?" His booming voice entered the air space, and I stumbled back in surprise. He rarely spoke, and I'd forgotten how far his deep voice projected.

I lifted my chin, regaining my composure. "Yes, of course I do. I saw that coming months ago. But I need to know if you can offer me protection."

Ever so slowly, the corners of his mouth spread almost ear to ear. "I sure can."

"That's what I thought. You be careful now." I stepped back into my entryway and closed the door on his unmoving body, decorated with his steady smile.

Instead of going back to the couch, I took the vial and arranged three candles on my living room floor, sprinkling herbs between them to create a protective line. Without it, I could be pulled into places I didn't wish to go.

Tiptoeing over the line of herbs, I lit each candle, holding the vial in my lap. With my hands spread out above me, I called out to the only one who could provide the assistance I needed.

"Papa Legba, you have provided me with what I need. You have believed in my path. But the path is winding, and I need answers now. How do I end this?"

I would not let this go on any longer than was absolutely necessary.

Or until my mission was finished.

# 12

The bag of Chinese food was warm in Charli's hand. An aroma of orange glaze floated into the air, and a rumbling began from deep within Charli's stomach.

She'd been so busy with research that she and Matthew had worked right through dinner, and now she was famished. Charli set the Chinese food down on the countertop and opened up the bag that contained a box of chow mein and another with orange chicken. She stopped by the utensil drawer to grab a fork before taking her dinner into the living room.

Charli plopped the food down on the living room coffee table but chose to sit on the floor. Although the soft electric-blue couch her grandmother had bought in another decade was in front of the coffee table, she didn't like to sit on it while she ate. It was a unique piece, and she didn't want to wreck it. And, of course, she wouldn't sit on the loveseat in the sitting room, Priscilla, without layers of bubble wraps upon her person.

Normally, she'd pick a book to read as she chowed down, but Charli was so ravenous, she started eating before she could go to the bookshelf. She'd only recently finished the biography on John Wayne Gacy and had to pick out something new.

*But what?*

She moseyed over to the bookshelf, the box of orange chicken still in hand, and glanced at the collection between bites. For once, none of the books sparked her interest. And Charli hated to do rereads because she retained information well and could remember the content of nearly every book.

How could she spend a rare quiet evening at home?

On one of the retro Papasan chairs was her laptop, plugged into the charger. It had gone untouched for a week. Charli often neglected her personal computer when she had a heavy case, and she'd had several in recent months.

But she hadn't been able to get Matthew's story from earlier out of her head. Curious, she searched the internet to see if she could find the published story.

There was so much more information than Matthew had told her. Yes, some had used the puffer fish to "raise" people from the dead, but other drugs could make people act like zombies.

One man had been "zombified" for nearly two years with a wide variety of drugs. The purpose, unlike with the puffer fish, was not to appear to raise the dead but to learn how to control someone's mind. If a drug enabled someone to harness another person's free will, they could create an army of people to do their bidding.

Charli tried to cross-reference some of the drugs in the paper with other studies but to no avail. There wasn't an abundance of scholarly articles about voodoo religion, which didn't surprise Charli.

She couldn't let this go, though. It was all so interesting. Instead of researching scientific studies, she started searching for anecdotal accounts of voodoo traditions. Most of them didn't involve any mention of drugs but instead referenced people who had witnessed a variety of spells and curses.

One woman posted on Reddit about how her aunt had used drugs to curse all her niece's ex-boyfriends. Each boyfriend had succumbed to death less than a year after the curse had been placed. It was likely just a coincidence, but it was an odd one.

In another case, a young man swore he had been in contact with his great-grandparents, and they had advised him on what career path would make him the most money. He swore he was a millionaire now and advised others on spells that would summon Papa Legba. Evidently, one needed to bring Legba a sacrifice to commune with the spirit world, and coming empty-handed could result in a person being pulled down to the underworld, never allowed to return.

Nearly an hour had passed when Charli checked her watch and discovered how much time she'd wasted with these searches.

*This wasn't research. It was all about the paranormal aspects of voodoo.*

As interesting as that may be, it wouldn't help Charli with her case. To think, she had chastised Matthew earlier for googling old voodoo stories, and now she was doing the same damn thing.

She shut her laptop and folded the empty Chinese food boxes on the table. Rising to her feet, she picked up both to take them to the kitchen trash.

*Buzzzzz.*

Her phone vibrated on the countertop next to the garbage can as she opened the lid. She turned the volume up as she checked the screen.

*You forget about me?*

The text was from Preston Powell. Charli's face warmed, and she was grateful nobody was around to see the blush on her cheeks. Of course, they were supposed to make plans for a date this weekend. She had failed to reach out.

But this was exactly what she was trying to tell Matthew earlier. How could she date anyone when her work life was this busy? She didn't have time to go out on dates and talk on the phone. Hell, she barely had any time to herself.

*I promise, I didn't forget. Just haven't had time to reach out.*

His response was immediate: *I'm just teasing. I figured Ruth had you assigned to the big zombie case. She seems to give you all the important cases, and rightfully so.*

*And rightfully so?* Charli's insides warmed at the compliment.

There was perhaps no better compliment for Charli to receive. She never had much of a reaction to men complimenting her looks. After all, she was born this way and didn't do anything to achieve her physical attributes, such as they were.

But her job was something she had worked at for years, and her skills as a detective were a point of pride. Charli grinned at her phone screen like a lovesick schoolgirl, but she couldn't help it. It had been so long since a man had complimented her on anything she actually cared about.

*Yep, Ruth has Matthew and me on the case.* Charli made sure her reply was neutral.

She feared being flirtatious with Preston, though she wasn't sure why. Preston was cute. He was obviously interested, and it had been a year since Charli had gone on a date. What was wrong with being forward?

Except she had this nagging feeling that going out with Preston wouldn't be just a date. Charli had never had a serious relationship, only flings. And flings didn't scare her, so she wouldn't mind having a fling with the sexy agent. But already, he was making her blush, and she feared she could develop real feelings for him.

*You'll just have to let me know once you've got some time. I'll be in town for at least a few more weeks.*

Charli's shoulders relaxed. That was right, Preston didn't live in Savannah. That meant things with them could never get too serious. A long-distance relationship would never work for Charli, not with how busy her career kept her. Even a short-distance relationship seemed impossible to manage.

She typed a response. *I will. I promise.*

Charli stifled a yawn. She might as well go to bed since she'd likely have to be up early to interview Carl Perkins. As she drifted off to sleep, images of Preston floated in her mind.

*They were laughing and sipping wine, a band playing a soft tune in the background.*

*"Dance with me, Charli."*

*"I'd love to."*

*She swayed to the music, enjoying Preston's arms around her and the way his eyes lit up when he looked into hers. She took a long, slow breath, inhaling his spicy scent. It had been way too long since she'd been out with a man. Why didn't she do this more often?*

*The music morphed into a lively beat. Charli twirled around, the music getting louder and louder. She clasped her hands to her ears.*

*What the hell?*

The crowd faded, and she jolted upright in her bed. Her cell phone was ringing. She fumbled in the dark, making contact with the source of the noise.

"Hello?" Charli stretched, rubbing the sleep from her eyes. She was so groggy, she forgot to identify herself as Detective Cross when she answered.

Of course, when she'd anticipated an early morning interview, she was thinking more like breakfast hours. Charli wasn't expecting her phone to ring by her bedside at two in the damn morning.

"Sorry to wake you, Detective Cross. It's Dr. Wu. I wasn't expecting you to answer. I had been planning to leave you a voicemail."

She went from semi-unconscious to on her feet in an instant. "No, it's fine. Go ahead."

"Carl Perkins is now awake and surprisingly alert. I wanted to let you know that we'd be holding him for observation until at least tomorrow night. You're free to interview him during visiting hours. They start at seven a.m."

*Visiting hours didn't apply to her.* She didn't say that, though. There was no point in arguing. She'd made up her mind.

"Thank you, Dr. Wu."

"You're welcome."

As soon as she hung up, she pulled up Matthew's number. Charli considered going on her own, but he'd be irritable the next day if she didn't invite him along.

"Charli, what the hell? It's two-freaking-thirty." Apparently, he was going to be irritable regardless.

"I know, but Carl Perkins is awake, and I want to go interview him." She was already pulling off her sleep shirt and reaching for a fresh blouse. "Do you want to go? I'm happy to do this on my own so you can get your beauty sleep."

Matthew groaned. "All right, fine, but you're driving."

# 13

The nurse slammed her chart on the white laminate countertop, muttering something Charli couldn't hear as she and Matthew approached.

"Detectives, were you not told to return during visiting hours?" She pushed her blonde bangs out of her face.

"Unfortunately, this is far more urgent than that. We need to speak with him. Now."

Charli spread her feet and jammed her fists on her hips, hoping to resemble a solid wall. She was not going to budge on this. She'd driven all the way here at three in the damn morning. Matthew was still wiping the sleep from his eyes. No way were they going home without speaking to their victim.

The nurse tapped her foot impatiently before shaking her head. She let out an exaggerated sigh. "Fine, follow me."

Charli and Matthew accompanied her down the hall until they reached room 168. When it swung open, the man in the bed was an entirely different person than the slack-jawed zombie from the cemetery.

There was nothing creepy about him now, a soft smile

playing on his lips. No, maybe "smile" wasn't the right word for it. There was sadness in his hazel eyes, a quiver to his lip despite his expression.

"Carl, two detectives are here to talk to you about what happened. But if you're not feeling up to it, you can tell them to come back later." The edge in the nurse's voice clarified that was what she preferred him to do.

But Carl shook his head. "No, that's fine. I'm okay to talk now. I'd love some help in figuring this all out."

The nurse gave one curt nod before exiting the room.

Charli stepped closer to the patient, pasting as friendly of a smile as she could muster on her face. "Mr. Perkins, I'm Detective Cross, and this is my partner, Detective Church. Do you remember us from yesterday?"

Carl drew a breath and released it slowly. "No, I'm sorry. I remember nothing from yesterday. My last memory was of leaving my house Sunday morning for church service."

"Do you remember getting to the church?" Matthew pulled up two chairs from the corner of the room for Charli and himself.

Carl scrubbed a hand over his face and blinked eyes that almost looked too weary to stay open. "I don't."

"Did anyone go to church with you?" Charli sank into the chair Matthew offered, although she was starting to believe they wouldn't be sitting there long. Carl didn't seem to have much information.

"No. I go to church alone now. I'm not married, been divorced for nearly a decade. Used to go with my son but... but I don't now."

A tear trickled down Carl's face, and Charli reached for the tissue box on the bedside table and handed it to him. "Have you ever had a memory loss experience like this before?"

Carl shifted in his hospital bed. The shoulders of his stiff gown were riding up whenever he moved.

"I'm old, Detective, but not that old. Nothing like this has ever happened to me. In my younger years, my friends used to describe blacking out when drinking, but I never experienced that. And I'm not much of a drinker anymore."

"You say you're not a drinker, but what about drug use?" Matthew leaned forward. "Did you take any drugs yesterday?"

"No, I wouldn't do that. I mean, not on purpose, but..." Carl's eyes shifted between Charli and Matthew. Shaky fingers tapped the edge of his hospital bed. The poor man was ready to jump out of his skin.

"Carl, we aren't here to arrest you for drug use. We are investigating a much more severe crime and believe you can be of help." Charli assumed this was causing his nervousness and wanted to reassure him.

The older man nodded, a faint smile pulling at his lips. "I definitely took nothing myself. But the doctor told me they found a drug in my system, something I never heard of. Curare, I think they said."

Matthew gripped the edge of his seat. "Did he give you any other details?"

"No. Apparently, they don't know when I took it, other than it had to be at some point yesterday. They ran other tests, gave me scans to see if I'd had a stroke, but there was nothing. Just that drug." The once gentle tears were a waterfall now. "But why? Why would someone do that to me? The doc said it can kill you if you take too much of it."

Charli had no words of consolation to offer, even if she were good at comforting people, which she wasn't. It had to be rough, not only losing one's memory but knowing someone intended to cause intentional harm.

Matthew stepped in, and Charli was glad that he was so

aware that she struggled with this part of an interview. "We are going to do our best to find out who was responsible."

Carl only nodded, wiping the tears from his face.

"You should rest. I know you've given us everything you remember, but please, if your memory returns, call us." Charli placed her card on the empty bedside table.

"Thank you, Detective. I will."

Charli stepped out into the hallway and waited for Matthew to close the door behind them. "What are your thoughts? Think he's telling the truth?"

Matthew shrugged. "I mean, it makes little sense for anyone to voluntarily take curare. And he appears genuinely devastated about everything that happened."

"I'm thinking the same thing. But I was really hoping we'd have more to go on after talking to him. Seems we know more about the past twenty-four hours than he does."

"Detective Cross?" A man in a white coat, Dr. Wu she presumed, was stalking up the hallway, a frown on his face. "I didn't think I'd see you until later in the morning."

She gave him a friendly smile. "Dr. Wu, hello. Sadly, this case is urgent, and we needed to speak to Carl right away." Not that it had helped much.

"He told us he tested positive for curare?" Matthew stepped forward, even with Charli.

"He did, yes. Not a common drug. I actually had to have a nurse explain its origins to me."

"How did she know about curare?" Charli pulled out her notebook, prepared to write down any relevant information.

Dr. Wu slid his hands into his white lab coat. "Apparently, she is neighbors with a woman who owns a shop catering to voodoo practitioners and chats with her from time to time. The nurse is not into voodoo herself, but she finds the culture interesting. I can't say I blame her. Though I'm disturbed to see such a drug used to harm a patient."

Charli glanced at Matthew, assessing whether he'd heard of such a shop.

Matthew gave an almost imperceptible shake of his head. "Where is this shop located?"

"I'm not sure. I do know her neighbor's name is Mami Watu, and I believe her name is in the title of her shop. You could probably do a quick internet search for it."

Matthew was already pulling out his phone to do so, leaving Charli to finish questioning Dr. Wu. "And you found no other drugs in his system? All other tests came back clean?"

"Clean as a whistle. He's otherwise a very healthy man. If you'll excuse me, I'd like to check in on him." Dr. Wu stepped into Carl's room.

There was a silent moment while Matthew attempted to find information on Mami Watu. It gave Charli time to take in the sterile white walls, only interrupted by the occasional metal gurney along the hallway. The hospital didn't usually bother her when she had to drop by during the day for work, but it had a different vibe at night.

The only time she'd been to a hospital this late was when her mother was sick. That had been a harrowing time in Charli's life, not one she cared to revisit anytime soon. She was about to suggest they head out when Matthew flashed her his phone.

"Here it is, on the east side of town. Can't believe neither of us has ever heard of it. It must be a small shop since it looks tiny on the map."

"When does it open?"

"Looks like nine thirty. How about we try to get a few more hours of sleep before heading out there?"

She yawned. "Sounds like a plan."

# 14

Charli rubbed her eyes while keeping one hand on the steering wheel. They were burning from lack of sleep. Running to the hospital at two in the morning probably hadn't been the best idea, considering Carl had offered little useful information. She'd managed to catch a few extra hours after their visit, but it hadn't been nearly enough.

On the flip side, if she and Matthew hadn't run into Dr. Wu when they did and learned about his nurse's knowledge on curare from her voodoo-practicing neighbor, they wouldn't be on their way to Mami Watu's shop right now. If Mami Watu told her neighbor about curare, perhaps she had information on how to obtain it.

"Turn right up here." Matthew jabbed a finger in the direction she should go.

Still in a haze of morning grogginess, even though it was almost ten, Charli didn't answer. She simply pulled ahead to an empty spot in front of the store sign that read "Mami Watu's House of Voodoo" in bold, black lettering.

Charli had fully expected to walk into an eclectic, cluttered shop overflowing with witchy items and spell books.

Instead, she and Matthew entered what appeared to be a high-end boutique. If she didn't know better, she'd assume this was a fancy skin care store. It even smelled of lavender. The walls were white and well-lit, lined with poplar wood shelves.

Of course, instead of skin care items, there were potions and herbs showcased everywhere. But they had been laid out in beautiful vials and apothecary jars. Occasionally, a small doll sat on the edge of one of the shelves. But they weren't the rudimentary cloth dolls they'd observed on scene. These were far more aesthetically pleasing, dressed up with beads and smiling faces.

At the sound of the door chime, a smiling Haitian woman walked through a back doorway toward the checkout counter. A tiny woman, she was only an inch or two taller than Charli and alarmingly thin.

"Hello, welcome to my store. How may I be of service today?"

"Wait, are you Mami Watu?" Matthew's jaw had sagged, and he appeared to be just as confused as Charli felt.

Like the shop, Mami Watu was the exact opposite of what Charli had expected. Besides an exquisitely beaded necklace, she wasn't dressed in traditional Haitian clothing. The petite woman wore a white business suit, a black blouse underneath, and high heels that clicked against the white marble tile of her shop. If Charli hadn't done some research and discovered Mami was in her late fifties, she would have thought the woman was much younger.

"I sure am, at your service."

"Beautiful shop you have here." Though Charli wanted to butter her up so she wouldn't feel threatened when they started asking questions, the statement was also very true. "I didn't realize we had a voodoo shop in Savannah. Only found out this morning when the news of that voodoo murder went viral."

The shop owner's eyes went soft with empathy. "Isn't that a horrible thing? As soon as I heard, my heart sank. I can't believe anyone would use voodoo in that manner."

"So, you don't think voodoo magic is inherently harmful?" Matthew's tone wasn't accusing but curious.

Mami reached for a glass jar filled with herbs on a nearby shelf. "Of course not. I loathe that voodoo has been made out to be this malicious, dangerous practice. That isn't the voodoo I grew up with. My shop is here to promote healing and connection with our spiritual world." Her smile lit up with a passionate glow, but it dissipated when she spoke again. "I've tried very hard to positively impact the perception of voodoo in Savannah, but horrid women like Tany Speers and Dawn Rita Mollette go out and disrespect our religious principles."

"Tany Speers?" This was the second time someone had referenced that name. But when the librarian mentioned it, it sounded like a legend. To hear Mami Watu speak her name, it was as if she'd met her.

The shopkeeper removed the lid from the jar and lifted it to her nose before delicately inhaling its contents. "Yes, she's a loathsome woman. I can't say for sure, but there are rumors she poisons drug dealers and sells hallucinogens to addicts so they might stop using. An absolutely heinous way to affect your community, in my opinion. But I'm sorry, I'm getting off track. I'd love to help show you the more positive aspects of voodoo. Is there anything I can help you find?"

"Actually, you're already helping us. I'm Detective Cross, and this is Detective Church. We're working on investigating the cemetery homicide case."

At Charli's introduction, Mami Watu's passion dissolved.

In its place stood an astute businesswoman, pleasantly prepared to help aid in their investigation.

She set the jar back on the shelf, putting it in line with the others. "My apologies that I didn't realize this sooner. Of course, I'd love to help you find out who is responsible for this injustice."

"Do you actually know Tany Speers? Can you get us in touch with her?" Matthew rested his hand on the glass counter of the customer service desk.

Mami shook her head, her silver earrings dangling. "Oh, no, we haven't seen each other in well over a decade. She is careful to make sure I never find out her location. Tany and her goons stay far away from my shop and me . These days, she distances herself from everyone, from what I hear."

That would explain the mythical presence Tany Speers seemed to hold. Charli scribbled in her notebook. "And you mentioned another name. Was it Dawn?"

"Dawn Rita Molette, yes." Mami drew a breath and let it out slowly, pursing her lips. "Not nearly as despicable as Tany Speers, but not utilizing voodoo the way she should. She is the daughter of a Romanichal woman, Elena, and her Haitian husband, Johnny Molette. She comes into my shop fairly regularly, buying dolls and herbal items for her potions. I don't enjoy her presence, but I'm not going to turn down a regular customer."

Charli's gaze drifted to one doll sitting on the countertop next to the cash register. "What exactly don't you like about her?"

Mami put a hand over her heart and leaned forward, pausing before she spoke. "She's a spooky woman. Dawn lives just outside of Savannah, in one of the swampy areas in the middle of nowhere. She feeds on superstitious individuals, usually people who are too unstable to realize how crazy they are, sadly. She's also very ornery." Mami sniffed and turned her head, as though she'd smelled something foul. "I am overwhelmed by her negative presence the second she walks in the door. The fact is, you cannot scam unstable people without taking in some of that energy through voodoo practices. You get what you give."

Matthew pulled out his phone. "Got an address?"

"I don't know the exact address, but you'll find her out on Old Burn Road. She's in a blue shack of a house, paint chipping everywhere, string lights hung crooked on the trim of her roof. You can't miss it."

Charli shook off her tiredness in light of the information they had just gained. Mami Watu was a wealth of knowledge. Charli had no idea how they'd find other voodoo practitioners without her insight. Whether Tany or Dawn was involved with the murder at the cemetery, there was no way to prove it at this point, of course. But it seemed they had strayed into the dark side of voodoo and should at least be able to provide information on where curare was attained.

Charli doubted Mami had any information on how to find illicit drugs, considering the quality of her business, but she had to ask, anyway. "Are you familiar with curare?"

Mami ran her hand along the edge of a blue silk scarf. "Of course I am. Never touched the stuff myself, but it's a frightening little drug. Not that I'd ever have need to harm someone, but even if I did, I'd never use curare."

Matthew grabbed a small jar of herbs on the counter. He crinkled his nose at the smell. "Why not?"

"It's extremely volatile. If one were to use it to poison someone else, they'd better be properly educated. Simply handling it can lead to you poisoning yourself if you proceed to touch your eyes, nose, or mouth afterward. You have to be extremely careful as accidental ingestion is common."

This was information that even Soames hadn't provided.

"Thank you for being so helpful. But I wonder if you

couldn't help us with one more bit of information?" Charli reached into her pocket for her phone.

The woman placed a hand on her chest in a welcoming gesture. "I would be happy to help in any way I can."

"Have you ever sold any dolls that look like this?" Charli pulled up a photo of the victim's hands.

Mami reared back, almost as if she'd been physically slapped. "No, I would never sell such a cheap version of a voodoo doll. That is the kind you'd find at some tourist booth in South America. I think you can buy them at online shops as well. I put a lot of care into my dolls, as you can probably tell." She pulled the nearest doll off the shelf and set it on the table. "I wish I could help you further, but I don't sell mass-produced items. I make all my dolls myself. My shop focuses on authenticity over quick profits."

"Understood. Well, that's all the information I think we need for now." Charli glanced at Matthew, giving him room to ask any other questions, but he remained silent. "Thank you for being so helpful."

"Of course. I hope you find whoever is responsible, so they're off the streets and cease using voodoo to harm others."

"We hope so as well."

Admittedly, coming to Mami Watu's shop had shifted Charli's views on voodoo a bit. Some individuals were practicing their magic in harmless ways. Charli may not believe in it, but as Matthew had mentioned, it didn't seem to be all bad.

Charli reached for the doorknob when Mami called out to her. "Detective Cross, feel free to come back during your off-hours. I can see something special in your eyes. I'd love to offer you a free reading."

Charli spun around. She wanted to brush it off and

opened her mouth to decline, but what came out instead was, "I'd love to."

*I'd love to?*

The words were foreign to her, as though her brain hadn't formed them. But she shook it off and exited before she could say something equally foolish.

"You want to get a psychic reading?" Matthew stared at his partner as if she were a stranger.

"Who knows?" She lifted a shoulder in a casual shrug. *Nothing to see here, folks.* "Maybe it'll be good for the case. I can do more research into this crazy shit."

But even as she said it, Charli knew this was a rationalization for an acceptance she couldn't explain.

## 15

Charli absorbed the chilling beauty of the swampland on Old Burn Road as she drove. It wasn't often that something could be both eerie and pleasant.

The street had become the residential neighborhood of Savannah outcasts, people who were too poor to live within city limits. There were many addicts out here as well as mentally unwell individuals who were unable to work typical jobs. It made sense that Dawn Rita would have a lot of business out here if she were in the game of scamming the downtrodden.

"Even in the morning, it feels darker out here somehow, huh?" Matthew shuddered as he glanced at his partner.

"Why is that? Is it cloudier out here or something?"

"I don't know, but it's definitely more humid."

Along the side of the road was a series of old, ramshackle houses. The kind of homes that would be condemned in the Savannah city limits yet were allowed to continue standing out here. Windows were boarded up. Porches had hazardous holes. Nobody could afford to fix even the most basic issues, and none of the neighbors cared.

"Is that it?" Matthew nodded at a blue house toward the end of the road.

"Looks like the string lights Mami Watu was talking about."

Charli pulled up the driveway. She normally loathed her work pants in the summer, but today she was grateful for them as she tried to walk through the overgrown grass. The last thing she needed was a tick bite in the middle of such an important investigation.

Matthew was the first to knock on the decrepit, faded blue door. On the porch was a metal bench covered in rust. The floorboards whined underneath Charli's midnight black boots.

"You think she's home?" Matthew knocked once more.

As if to answer, half a face peaked through the space as the door cracked open. "Hello?"

"Hi, I'm Detective Cross. This is Detective Church. We're looking for a Dawn Rita Molette?"

"This is her." The eye narrowed into a thin slit. "What do you want?"

Now, this was more what Charli had been expecting when she visited Mami Watu. A suspicious woman. "We need to ask you a few questions. Can we come inside?"

"No!" Dawn pushed her body through the opening. "We can talk out here. Do you want sweet tea? Here, sit over there. I'll go get sweet tea."

Dawn had moved back inside before either of them had a chance to answer. A sigh escaped Matthew as he walked over to the bench and sat down, patting the seat next to him.

"You want me to sit on that?" Charli wrinkled her nose. She couldn't even sit on Priscilla, the loveseat from hell in her own sitting room. She did not mess with questionable furniture.

Matthew shrugged. "It's metal. What could go wrong?"

Charli tossed her head in the direction of the wooden porch boards. "You're kidding, right? I think if we add our combined weight to that thing, we'll be meeting the ground below within seconds." Not to mention the fact that Charli wasn't up-to-date on her tetanus shot.

She instead chose to stand near the door, which soon opened. Dawn returned with a tray holding three sparkling clean glasses of sweet tea and a plate filled with some type of pastry.

As poor as the house indicated she was, Dawn appeared to be meticulously neat and tidy.

"Potato cake?" Dawn offered the baked goods to the detectives before reaching for one herself.

Matthew shook his head. "No thanks, but I'll happily take that tea. It's brutal out here today."

Charli had reservations about consuming anything from people she didn't know. But she'd forgotten to grab her water bottle on the way out today and hadn't had a thing to drink since she left the house.

The tea looked tempting, and Dawn was allowing her to choose which to take among the three. In her experience, that indicated nothing dangerous had been added.

Plus, Matthew was right. It was far more humid out here in the swamps. Beads of sweat were forming on Charli's temples. She accepted the glass closest to Dawn and sniffed the contents before taking a tiny sip. When nothing tasted funny and her vision didn't blur, she took another equally small sip.

"It's lovely to have visitors, even if you are the law." Dawn's eyes darted around, and Charli suspected their hostess was not sober.

It would explain her sudden change in demeanor and why she refused to allow them to come inside the house. But they weren't here for a drug bust, and even if they were, they didn't have the proper warrants to demand entry. Technically, Dawn wasn't required to speak with them, and Charli wasn't about to scare her off.

"Dawn, we were hoping you might be able to help us with a case we're working on. We've been told you visit Mami Watu's shop to buy voodoo dolls."

Dawn shoved the last bite of potato cake in her mouth, chewing and swallowing before answering. "Oh, yeah, but not often. She's really expensive. I only go to her when I have a customer, and I'm out of stock. I buy most of my dolls online, and then I paint 'em to match the description my client wants."

"You sell these dolls?" Matthew took another sip of his sweet tea.

Charli did the same. It was actually delicious, with just the right amount of sugar.

Dawn reached up to smooth her wavy dark hair. "Yes, I sure do."

"Have you ever sold one to Carl Perkins or Jefferson Brown?" Charli watched closely to gauge her reaction.

But she didn't try to hide it. "Carl Perkins, yep. Not to Jefferson, though. Why you askin'?"

"Have you heard about the voodoo cemetery homicide? And the zombie man walking outside the cemetery gates?" Matthew plunked his glass down on the bench next to him.

Their hostess reached for her own glass on the nearby railing and took a long gulp before setting it back down. "No. Sorry, I don't get out much. And I don't watch much TV, either."

"Well, Mr. Perkins was drugged and left wandering just outside that cemetery holding a voodoo doll. He's pretty distraught and has no memory of what happened." Charli observed as, for a moment, Dawn stopped fidgeting, and her mouth drooped into a deep frown.

"Oh, no. That is no good, no good at all. Is he all right?"

"He's going to be okay. But it would help us greatly to know why he bought the doll."

Dawn rubbed her arms briskly, her hands settling at the hem of her worn tunic. "I don't ask. Ain't my business what they do with it. That's personal."

"Would you happen to know where to get curare?" Matthew rose from his seat.

Charli wished he had chosen another moment to stand. With his height, he could be intimidating. Now, Charli didn't know if Dawn was in a tizzy from the question or Matthew's body language. But Charli could be sure of one thing. Dawn was uncomfortable now. She started scratching at her thighs.

"No, of course not. I don't even know what that is."

Charli raised her eyebrows at her partner. If Mami Watu, an esteemed businesswoman, was aware of curare, surely living out on Old Burn Road, Dawn would have at least heard of it. But if Dawn was privy to more than she let on, she wasn't going to share.

"What about Tany Speers? Do you ever work with her?" Charli sipped the last of her tea.

"Work with...Tany?" Dawn squinted at the detectives and massaged her neck. "Who told you about Tany? Was that Mami Watu?"

Charli was quiet, not wanting to confirm or deny this information. But Dawn seemed to understand what that silence meant.

Dawn was visibly agitated, pacing back and forth on the dilapidated porch. "You cannot trust that woman. You can't. Don't believe a word she says about anything, especially Tany."

"So, you don't work with Tany?" Matthew pressed.

Dawn threw her arms in the air, shaking her head from

side to side. "No! No, I ain't ever worked with her or Mami Watu. Now, I think I gotta go."

This was what Charli feared would happen. But there was no way around it. Their questions were bound to spook her at some point. It was still helpful to learn she'd somehow been involved with Carl's voodoo doll. And her hesitance to continue speaking was information in and of itself.

Charli handed Dawn the empty glass as well as her card. "Thank you for the tea. If you remember any other useful information, please call."

"Sure thing. I…" Dawn froze as the tips of her fingers met Charli's.

Charli glanced down at Dawn's hand. "Is everything all right?" The other woman was gripping the business card so hard, it crumpled.

"Y-yes." Dawn's expression transitioned from frightened to concerned. "You feeling okay, ma'am?"

That wasn't the reaction Charli was expecting. "Uh, I'm fine. Why?"

"I dunno. You seem…marked." There was an edge to that word.

Adrenaline dumped into Charli's system. Not only from the word but from the way Dawn Rita's expression had changed once again. Her face had grown hard, her dark eyes like bullets.

*What the hell was she talking about? Was this some kind of threat? An insinuation that if Charli investigated further, Dawn would come after her?*

Matthew drew himself to his full height, taking a step forward. But Charli cut him off before he could open his mouth.

"If I'm marked, and if anything happens to me, you can guarantee that my partner will come back here and burn down this little shack you call a home. Do you understand me?"

Dawn jumped back, dropping the glass. It hit one of the bench legs and shattered, sending shards flying.

"I-I'm real sorry. Sorry." Dawn scurried back into her house, slamming the door behind her.

A chill ran down Charli's spine.

*What the hell had Dawn Rita meant?*

## 16

Matthew fumbled with a wrinkle in his shirt. His partner was gripping the steering wheel so hard, the edges of her knuckles were white. She hadn't communicated with him their next step in the investigation but had simply started the car and begun driving. They'd been silent since they left Dawn's house. And he had no idea how to break that silence.

Frankly, it was taking all his focus to process what the hell had just happened. In all the years he'd worked with Charli, he had never seen her lash out at a suspect, and she'd dealt with some twisted characters over the course of her career. Sociopaths that made Dawn Rita seem as harmless as a fly.

Hell, Dawn Rita very well might be as harmless as that particular insect. The woman was an addict, no disputing that, but many people who lived out here in the swamps were. That was no surprise. But Matthew wasn't even convinced that Dawn had been threatening Charli. Her comment had seemed more of a consequence of her paranoid thinking than anything else.

Matthew didn't want to bring it up, but it was the elephant in the car. There was almost never any awkwardness between them, and he wasn't interested in starting that now. But, dammit…

"What was that about?" The words flew from his lips before he could continue to overthink the situation.

"What?"

He knew Charli was playing coy, but she didn't pull off coy very well. "You snapping at Dawn Rita like that. You can't just go threatening witnesses, Charli."

Charli groaned. "I know, okay? Of course, I know that." The muscles popped in her jaw before she exhaled a long sigh. "I'm not sure what happened. It just came over me like a wave. The way she was looking at me when she said it set me off."

"You think her stare was sinister?" Matthew hadn't gotten that at all from her eyes. Dawn struck him as more confused than anything.

"I don't know. Maybe I was reading too much into it. Look, I'm tired." As if to prove her level of exhaustion, she yawned so big her back molars were on view. "We had a crazy night, and it's been back-to-back cases. I'm just not feeling like myself today. I can't explain it."

That much Matthew understood. Stress could do crazy things to a person. Matthew knew that better than anyone.

"Try to relax. Maybe you should go home for the rest of the day. I can continue with the investigation and—"

"No!" Charli pointed a finger in his direction, her gaze never leaving the road. "No, I'm fine. I'm going to follow up on this case. It's important. We both know Ruth wants this wrapped up fast, and I'm not going to disappoint her."

Charli's words failed to comfort Matthew. Ignoring stress so you didn't disappoint others was almost never a good idea.

"Okay, well, if you need a break, the offer is on the table."

Matthew would not argue it any further. When Charli wanted to be stubborn, there was no stopping her. The more Matthew told her to relax, the more she'd dig in her heels.

He'd give her a break on this. There was no reason to rub salt in the wound. "I think we can go to the Rising Moon next. Sound good to you?"

"Perfect." But Charli's flat tone didn't scream any such thing.

Matthew did his best to ignore it. "What do you think about Carl Perkins buying a voodoo doll? Because I'm thinking it makes him look extremely suspicious."

Charli ran her fingers through her hair. "You think so?"

"You don't?" That was surprising. Charli usually caught onto a trail of clues long before Matthew did.

She yawned again, less dramatically this time. "I'm just still kind of tired. I haven't had time to think about it. Why don't you run me through your thought process?"

"Well, he could have bought the doll that looks like Jefferson. Maybe he even bought some curare from Dawn, though she'll never admit to that. He was trying to kill Jefferson in the cemetery and then ended up drugging himself by accident because he wasn't careful enough. Just like Mami said."

Charli nodded. "Except Carl wasn't in the cemetery to begin with, remember? He was first walking up the street before we got to him."

"Mami said you had to touch the drug to your eyes, nose, or mouth to get high. Maybe he started walking home, rubbed his nose or eyes, and got high before he could arrive. In his hazy state, he started wandering back to the last place he was, the cemetery."

It made sense to Matthew. The second voodoo doll could have been an extra, perhaps someone else Carl had been after. Or it was intended to stay on Carl's person as a red herring, making both him and Jefferson look like victims of the same perpetrator.

Either way, the next item on their investigation was to figure out if there was any conflict between Carl Perkins and Jefferson Brown.

Charli tapped the steering wheel with her thumbs. "Do you want to head to the hospital before going to the Rising Moon?"

"No, let's give him some time to rest. Besides, maybe someone at the bar will know about any tension between them. Then we can grill Carl about it to apply some pressure."

"Sounds good."

Something felt off. It wasn't normal for Charli to be so passive in planning their investigation. That was her strong suit. She was handing over the reins to Matthew, something she hadn't done since their first case together. And hell, she hadn't even handed over the reins then. It was more like playing tug-of-war with them, struggling to let Matthew lead while she was eager for her first investigation.

But maybe she was just tired. The back-to-back cases had been exhausting for Matthew too, and he at least got to have a couple days off—if you could call flying across the country to be ignored by your teenage daughter time off—in the middle of them. Charli hadn't taken a vacation since she became a detective.

They sat in silence for the rest of the ride to the Rising Moon. And inside the bar, it was equally quiet.

It made sense for a Tuesday afternoon. There were only two men at the bar sifting through a pile of paperwork.

"Excuse me, sirs, can you point me to someone in charge of this establishment?" Matthew propped his elbow on the edge of the bar top.

Even in the middle of the day, it was dark inside. The

windows were small, and the walls were painted black, lined with various graffiti.

"Guess I can say that's me, Bob Anker. I'm one of the... uh...the owner. Who's asking?" Bob twisted in his chair, causing a wrinkle to form in his navy t-shirt. When he moved in his seat, Matthew could better see the tears in his jeans.

Not exactly the kind of guy you'd expect to be the owner of any establishment, but with the Rising Moon, it was par for the course.

"I'm Detective Church, and this is my partner, Detective Cross. We're investigating the death of Jefferson Brown. And you are?" Matthew glanced at the other man.

"Leland Finch, but I'm no owner, just an employee. So I guess I'll get going." Leland rose from his stool, but Matthew put up a hand to stop him.

"That's fine, actually. You take a seat right there. We'd love to talk to anyone who knew Mr. Brown."

The two men glanced at each other but acquiesced. Matthew grabbed two barstools and pulled them up across from the guys. Charli slid onto one while Matthew took the other.

Matthew addressed the owner. "You said you own this establishment. Does that mean you co-owned this place with Jefferson?"

"That's right."

Matthew leaned forward. "Do either of you know if Jefferson had any beef with a guy named Carl Perkins?"

"Doesn't ring a bell." Leland's tone was terse. He clearly didn't want to talk to the cops.

Bob nodded in agreement. "I'm not familiar with the name, either."

Charli smacked her notebook on the bar top. "Is anything

going to ring a bell for you guys, or do you plan to remain difficult?"

Her voice sent a jolt through Matthew. Once again, it was oddly aggressive. Was she really this annoyed so early in the conversation?

Bob folded his arms. "We probably won't know much, no."

Charli's lips tightened, frustration oozing from her. "Yeah? I wonder, on any given weekend, how much money would you lose if you couldn't push narcotics at this bar?"

"Excuse me?" Bob played with his watch.

"You heard me. If my partner and I showed up every weekend to ask questions, how many of your patrons would head right out the door?"

Despite her anger, this wasn't a bad tactic. Matthew could get used to aggressive Charli.

Bob sighed. "All right, sure, cops sniffing around is not good for business. But all that drug shit, that was Jefferson's game, not mine. I've been trying to clean this place up for years. Now that he's gone, I might actually have a chance to make this a decent bar. I don't want to own a dive any longer. It's too much trouble."

"If you want to run a decent bar, it wouldn't hurt to help out a couple of detectives investigating a homicide, huh?" Matthew planned to play nicer than Charli. It wouldn't be the first time they'd played good cop, bad cop, though Matthew was often cast in the bad cop role.

Bob uncrossed his arms, playing with a tear in his jeans. "Fine. But I was being honest. I don't know any Carl. Do you, Leland?"

The employee shook his head and drummed his fingers on the bar top, glancing at the stack of papers. "No, never heard of him."

"Does Jefferson have any enemies who might try to cause

him harm?" Charli's eyes shot daggers at the men. She meant business.

Bob laughed. "Are you kidding? He had a ton. If the man was good for anything, it was making enemies."

"Any actual death threats?" Matthew kept his face neutral.

"Sure, I don't know from who, but he kept getting letters in between his windshield wipers that talked about his time coming to an end. Jefferson never told us who it was specifically. Just that it was a guy who blamed him for killing his kid." Bob glanced at Leland. "Did you know his name?"

"Nope."

Charli opened her mouth, but Matthew beat her to the question. "Wait, did you say Jefferson killed someone?"

*Didn't they think that required a little explanation?*

Bob shrugged. "I mean, yeah, Jefferson killed a lot of people if you wanna get technical. He's not a murderer, but he's a drug dealer. Whoever the guy's son was, he overdosed. I guess Jefferson was his dealer."

Bam! There it was, the motive for Carl Perkins having done the deed. Matthew glanced at Charli, but she had little reaction.

"We'd like a list of employees so we can ask again to see if anyone can confirm an identity for the man threatening Jefferson."

Bob didn't look pleased but nodded. "You can try, but don't expect much."

The detectives stood, and before he could deliver a proper goodbye, Matthew's phone started vibrating in his pocket. "Excuse me. I have to take this."

He pushed the barstools back before moving outside to put Ruth on speakerphone. "Detective Church."

"Just wanted to give you a heads-up that the hospital is about to discharge Carl Perkins. You two have spoken to him, right?"

Matthew huffed. "We did, but we've got a lot more questions now."

"You better head to the hospital before he has a chance to go home. We don't want to give him time to get his story straight or hide evidence."

"Right, we'll be right over." Charli was already getting into the driver's seat of her little hybrid.

Fortunately, the hospital was only about ten minutes away. But ten minutes was long enough to call an Uber home. Time was of the essence. As always.

# 17

Adrenaline coursed through Charli's veins as she raced to the hospital. If Matthew was right, and evidence suggested he was, then any time that Carl had to himself was a risk to their investigation.

Right as they pulled into the parking lot, Carl was stepping out of the hospital's front door. He was wearing the filthy clothes he'd had on at the cemetery, blinking as he stepped into the sunlight.

Charli pulled up in front of him, ready for a foot chase. He'd been cooperative in the hospital, but seeing the detectives again might be enough to set alarm bells ringing in his head.

"Carl!" Matthew got out of the passenger side and slammed the door.

Carl's eyes widened but not in fear. Instead, his face was awash with relief. "Detectives, I was hoping to see you again."

Their jaws dropped. It was Matthew who responded. "Carl, we're going to need you to come down to the precinct with us. We've got some questions."

Charli expected this might be the moment they finally received some resistance, but there was none.

"Okay, sure." Carl climbed into the back seat as soon as Matthew opened the door.

Admittedly, this was all a bit odd for a person of interest. But if he was going to make the trip to the station easy on them, Charli wouldn't question it.

When they got back to the precinct, they took Carl to an interrogation room, offering him a water bottle before they got started. After thanking them, he took a long, slow drink. He appeared to be worse for wear, still exhausted from the drugs and his hospital stay.

With the camera recording, Matthew started the interview by stating the date and the people present. "Carl, thank you for willingly coming with us to answer a few questions. We've got some new information we'd like to ask you about."

"I'd love any new information you can give me."

Carl straightened in his chair, eager to learn more about what had happened. It explained why he had no issue coming back to the precinct.

"Do you know Jefferson Brown?" Charli raised an eyebrow at her partner as the color drained from Carl's face.

"Yeah, I know him."

Charli kept her face neutral. "What is your relationship with him?"

Carl cleared his throat before answering. "I didn't know him well…only through my son."

"Have you had any problems with Mr. Brown in the past?" Charli decided there was no point in beating around the bush.

Carl's hazel eyes moved to the one-way window on the wall. "Yeah, I won't deny it."

"What happened?"

Carl drew in a long breath before slowly releasing it. "I've been leaving him notes, phone calls. Do you know what that man did to my son?"

Charli nodded. "We are aware of the content of your letters, yes."

"Then you understand why I did that." Carl lifted pleading eyes to Charli. "Look, I was angry. No, angry doesn't even begin to cover it. I hate that man, and I don't bemoan his death. I know he took away a lot more children than just my son. But I didn't do it. I'm not capable of killing anyone. I wanted to scare the guy. And sadly, I don't think it ever worked. He seemed unfazed by my threats."

Charli felt for the man, understanding a little of how he must feel. "Have any of your memories come back to you during your hospital stay?"

Carl rubbed his face with both hands, tracing a small scar on his neck with his finger. "None. I was hoping you guys had found something out and could help with the gaps in my mind. The only thing I remember is leaving my house, nothing else."

"The voodoo doll you had in your hand the morning we found you, did you purchase that?" Charli took out her phone to remind him of the image.

Carl leaned toward the phone from across the table. "No, I never bought that."

"Really?" Matthew pinned him with his gaze. "Because Dawn Rita Molette said you did buy it from her."

"She did?" He tapped his fingers against his temple as if doing so would jog loose his memory. "I-I don't remember that. I couldn't have…"

The detectives exchanged a glance. They could tell the gears were turning in Carl's head as he fidgeted with his hands.

"But you are familiar with Dawn Rita?" Charli scrutinized the older man's face.

Carl bit his lip. "Yeah, I've got family members that mess around with that stuff. I know Dawn, I know Mami Watu, but I don't do any of that. I swear. I'm a good Christian man. I don't worship nobody but the good Lord."

"Are you sure?" Charli tilted the phone toward him again. "Take a closer look at the doll. Maybe it'll spark something."

Just as Carl moved forward, a black flash came over the image. It disappeared entirely.

"What the hell?" Matthew took the phone from Charli's hand and started tapping buttons. "It won't turn back on."

Charli swallowed hard. *It was just a glitch, or maybe the battery simply died. Phones glitched all the time, right?* Except Charli had never seen anything like that. And the timing…?

"You all right?" Matthew put a hand on hers.

Charli jerked, snatching it away. "I'm fine. Let's stay on task. Carl, are you sure you have no idea where that voodoo doll came from?"

Carl shook his head and reached for his water bottle. "No. I'm sorry, Detectives. Everything is so hazy."

Charli processed through her options, deciding to head down the brutally straightforward route. "But the doctors cleared you. You had no head trauma. Your tests were all clean. It doesn't make sense that you wouldn't remember things you did days before this incident occurred. You understand why what you're saying doesn't seem believable, right?"

Carl's face crumpled. He lowered his face in his hands and began to sob. "I know. I know that. I can see it in your face. But I swear, I'm telling the truth. I want to help you! You have no idea how badly I want to help you. Something is wrong here, and I want to know what it is. I'm doing my best!"

While Carl's head was still in his hands, Charli nodded toward the door in a silent communication with her partner.

Matthew immediately stood. "Will you excuse us for a moment?"

Carl raised his head, swiping a hand across his face. "Uh huh, yeah."

Once in the observation room, Charli started to fidget with her phone. It turned back on as if nothing had happened, her battery showing at sixty-five percent.

Charli did her best to shake off that bizarre moment. "What are you thinking?"

Matthew leaned against the glass separating them from their shaken looking suspect. "I'm thinking if he's lying, get that man his Oscar nomination."

Charli couldn't disagree with that. "He does seem genuine, but we need to keep our options open. Hey, for all we know, the man spent a semester at Juilliard. He could be a talented actor." But even as she said the words, Charli wasn't convinced.

"Right. I'm going to see if I can turn up any more information about the death of his son. The more information we have, the better."

They both knew they didn't have enough to hold Carl against his will. They needed more or they'd have to cut him loose.

"Perfect, I'll help you." She focused on the man who looked so broken and sighed. "But first, let me check on him. I'll see if I can get him to stay willingly."

Charli entered the interrogation room, finding a more composed Carl sipping from his water bottle. "We're not going to hold you, but would you be willing to stay for a while?" He eyed his surroundings, and Charli read his mind. "We would put you in a room that's more comfortable, of course."

Carl nodded and rose from his chair. He was a tall man,

but now, he seemed to have shrunk several inches. "Sure, I'll stay. I want to get answers as bad as you do."

Once Carl was settled in another room, Charli rejoined her partner. "On second thought, you go ahead and check into the death of Carl's son. I'm going to visit Mami Watu."

Matthew's mouth fell open. "Uh, you are?"

"Yeah." Charli shrugged, hoping she appeared to be more casual about the offer than she felt. "Maybe she knows of some spell or curse that could impact memory like this."

He narrowed his eyes at her. "Okay, see. Now I know you really aren't feeling like yourself. Don't tell me you're buying into all this magic mumbo jumbo."

She scoffed so hard a bit of spittle flew from her mouth. "Of course, I don't believe in it. But that doesn't mean there aren't answers within some of this information. It may not be real, but the reasons people buy into it are very real."

Charli hadn't been able to get *The Serpent and the Rainbow* out of her head. That initially appeared to be some kind of magic when, in reality, there was a perfectly logical explanation.

Somewhere in this mess, there was rational reasoning. Charli only had to find it.

# 18

An unsettling air surrounded Charli as she stared at Mami's shop, willing herself to enter the building. But every time she reached for the car's door handle, she paused.

*Why didn't she want to go into the building? What was holding her back? What was she afraid of?* Charli wasn't sure. But she had to do her job. Whatever discomfort arose within her had to be stuffed down. She forced herself to open the door and strode into Mami's shop.

"Detective Cross, I didn't expect to see you back so soon." Mami Watu was shoveling herbs into a large jar when Charli stepped through the door.

"I wasn't expecting to be back so soon, either. And I hope you don't mind, but I have a few more questions for you. You've been a great help to our investigation. My partner and I aren't exactly experts in voodoo culture."

"Of course." Mami dusted away some loose herbs and put the lid on the jar. "Why don't we go into the back room. I can make you a cup of tea, and we can chat. I've been on my feet all day."

Charli flashed Mami the best smile she could muster. "That sounds great, thanks."

The back office was just as organized as the rest of the shop. There was no desk but instead a large coffee table surrounded by multiple chairs. A kettle of hot tea rested in the middle of the table with several empty cups.

"I often take my clients back here for readings. Tea leaves, card fortunes, not all of it comes from voodoo, but it's another hobby that supplements my income. Here, sit. I know it's a little hot outside for tea, but I keep the air-conditioning blowing so cold."

And that breeze was even stronger in the office. The table sat adjacent to a ceiling vent. The cushion was cold as ice, so Charli gratefully took the cup Mami poured her. She didn't even bother asking what was inside of it, though the tea had a pleasant minty scent.

Mami poured another cup for herself, and Charli waited for her to take the first sip of the tea. As she watched, Charli noticed just how thin the woman's arms were when the sleeve of her jacket rode up on her forearm. "What can I do for you, Detective?"

Charli took another sip of the liquid, inhaling the invigorating aroma before setting the cup down. "I was wondering what you could tell me about memory loss spells."

The shopkeeper reached for some tarot cards on her desk, straightening them before setting them down. "Well, there are plenty of charms to affect the memory. What do you specifically want to know? I've got a spell book I'm happy to go through with you."

Charli supposed there wasn't any benefit in that. She didn't need to learn the specifics of any spells. What she needed to know was if any of them could actually work. But how could she tactfully imply that she didn't believe any of this magic was real?

Charli crossed her legs, scooting back in her seat, and decided to just go for it. "I suppose what I'm asking is…can any of those spells actually work?"

Mami let out a short laugh and leaned back into her chair. "You're a nonbeliever, of course."

Charli suppressed a smile, not wanting to offend the other woman. "I am. I mean, I'm not superstitious at all. But that doesn't mean I don't acknowledge that the psychosomatic effect is real. Maybe if people believe that a spell has been put on them, they'll act accordingly."

Charli wanted to be as diplomatic as possible. She didn't want to turn Mami off to answering her questions. It wasn't like Charli thought voodoo, in particular, was fake. She just wasn't spiritual in general.

That wasn't by accident. Whenever Charli considered religion, her mind went to Madeline. She could analyze religion without wondering whether her spirit was out there somewhere. And that unsettled Charli deeply.

"Hmm." Mami nodded, her silver earrings swaying back and forth. "It's like anything else. How often have you seen a Christian pray and then get exactly what they want? I'm not a believer in God or Jesus. Like you probably look down on voodoo, I don't see the merit in that religion at all. But I don't deny that when someone prays, they set a course for their life in motion. Yes, the mind is a powerful thing. Faith can convince someone of anything, in my opinion."

Charli uncrossed her legs, sitting up straighter in her chair. "And you've seen it happen? I mean, you've seen someone experience a spell or curse and react to it authentically?"

Mami smiled, and Charli noted how her cheekbones jutted out. *This woman could seriously use a cheeseburger.*

"Yes, I certainly have. I wouldn't be in this line of work… in this calling…if I hadn't."

*Was it more than the curare impacting Carl's memory? Could he have been sent to buy that voodoo doll on a supposed curse, and his brain convinced himself it was real?* Not to mention the fact that the man had clearly gone through something traumatic during the time he'd forgotten. The trauma, in combination with a curse, could be enough for his mind to block out the events. Another possibility was that there was more than curare in his system.

Charli ran a finger around the rim of her cup. The simple white porcelain had delicate blue designs. "Do you know of any illicit drugs that would affect the body similar to the way curare does?"

Mami Watu took a sip of her tea. "The way curare does? No, I don't think so. Not any Haitian drugs, anyway. To be honest, I don't dabble in any of those illicit drugs. The worst drug I've ever sold is a mushroom stem that, in the wrong hands, could be considered a hallucinogen. But used as incense, it's quite pleasant. I only know so much about curare because of its reputation."

Silence ensued for a few moments, and Charli sipped more of her tea as she tried to piece this all together. Her hands gripping the warm porcelain cup calmed her. It was the most relaxed she'd been all day. But taking the edge off wasn't making the pieces fit together any better.

The shopkeeper stared hard at Charli, her gaze taking in the way the detective's hands fidgeted with the cup. "Something is bothering you, child."

Charli snapped back to attention. "No, I'm fine."

But Mami's gaze didn't falter as her wise dark brown eyes seemed to search Charli's soul. Charli decided it was best not to deny her the truth. The woman had a kind of sixth sense.

"I have been feeling a little off today."

A slight smile settled on Mami's cheeks. "How about we get you that reading we talked about, eh?"

This was a complete waste of Charli's time, but she was already sitting across from Mami Watu. The reading was free, and she'd been so helpful during the investigation. *Why not humor her?*

"Sure, okay."

"Are you done with that cup of tea?" Mami reached for it, and Charli slid it over.

"Oh, yes…"

Mami Watu tilted the cup under the light. "Give me your hands, Detective."

Charli obeyed. Mami flipped the younger woman's palms up and traced the lines with her nail.

Mami stared intently at Charli's hands. "You're a bit of a workaholic, aren't you?"

This bit of information didn't faze Charli. It didn't require a psychic to figure out a homicide detective worked most of the time. There wasn't a detective at the precinct who didn't work themselves to the bone. Even to those who were not aware Charli was a homicide detective, the bags under her eyes were a clear enough sign that she had no work-life balance.

"Yes, I am."

"You need to relax. Take a vacation. Focus on other aspects of your life." Mami Watu met Charli's gaze once again, taking another deep dive into the depths of Charli's soul. "But you can't for some reason."

Charli swallowed hard. She wasn't sure why this observation felt more personal. "No, I can't."

Mami slowly released Charli's hands. "And why is that?"

The air in the room seemed to grow thinner, taking all the saliva in Charli's mouth along with it. "I-I don't know."

"But you do." The assertion was delivered softly but with all the confidence in the world. "You are focused on another woman."

Charli threw her head back and let out a throaty chuckle. "Mami, I'm afraid you've got it all wrong. I'm not attracted to women."

Charli might not have spent the night with a man in quite a while, but it wasn't because she was seeking female company…not that there was anything wrong with that. At all.

Mami covered one of Charli's hands with her own, and the detective fought the urge to jerk it away. "Not like that, my dear. No, I don't see any romantic connection between the two of you. This feels more familial."

A woman Charli had a familial connection with. Could that be Ruth? They weren't exactly close outside work, but she was the only woman who came to mind. Perhaps, in some way, Charli viewed Ruth as a motherly figure. Not one that was very maternal, of course. But someone Charli looked up to and relied on for guidance.

Mami's hand flew to her chest, and she made a sound close to a gasp. "I see a clear picture now. She was like a sister to you, wasn't she?"

The air grew even thinner. "Who?"

"Madeline."

*Crash!*

Charli's chair sounded like a bullet coming from a gun when she bolted out of it so fast. Her mind spun in circles as she tried to process what she'd just heard.

"I-I'm sorry, I need to go."

"Oh, no, Detective!" Mami was on her feet as well, her necklace clinking with the sudden movement. "I had no intention of frightening you. I only wanted to—"

Charli didn't wait to hear another word.

Dashing through the door, Charli raced to her car, fumbling for her key fob. Her heart pounded hard in her chest, causing an unrelenting throb in her temples. The last thing she had expected was a near stranger to recite Madeline's name to her.

*How the hell could she know that?*

It wasn't like someone could google it. Sure, they could search for Madeline's murder, but nowhere would they be able to find a connection to Charli since Charli had also been a minor at the time. She had made sure of that by conducting numerous searches for her and Madeline's names multiple times online. Charli was careful about her privacy.

And if there was no connection to be found between Charli and Madeline, how did Mami know about her best friend? Did she know all about Madeline or only her name? Had Charli underestimated the supernatural world? Was there a chance that, somewhere within the real world, there were splashes of magic that could explain what had just happened in there? Was there some type of dark power at work?

Charli squeezed her eyes shut as she fought to regain her breath. She didn't want to consider those possibilities.

# 19

Matthew's teeth ground together like overworn gears on a rusty machine. He had clenched his jaw so hard that he couldn't relax the muscles. Not with the irritation that was coursing through him.

"Why can't we just hold him for a little longer?" He ran his fingers through his short hair, not even aware he was tapping his foot. "He's here willingly, after all."

Ruth's eyes shot daggers at Matthew. "Because of this little thing called public perception in addition to the fact that Mr. Perkins has doctor's orders to rest, Detective Church. You know as well as I do that we don't have enough information to hold him. You've got his story, and that's all you're going to get right now. There will be time to question him later."

"But he's our prime suspect."

Yes, Carl had been convincing, but Matthew had to go where the evidence went. Right now, the evidence was pointing to Carl Perkins.

"I'm aware of that, Detective. The doctors say that in addition to the curare they found in his bloodstream and his extreme fatigue, undue stress could be placed on his body without rest. He's not a young man, and the last thing I need right now is to be responsible for a medical event. I won't argue about it any longer. Go release him now."

Matthew bit his tongue and thrust his hands into his pockets. Once Ruth said she was finished with a conversation, Matthew would not dare continue it. But, dammit, he really needed more time to get more information about Carl's son.

He hadn't been able to find much. So far, all Matthew had discovered was a brawl he'd been taken in for at the Rising Moon. It helped to confirm that Carl's kid likely did buy drugs from Jefferson, but that link was already pretty clear.

There would still be time to do more research, of course. As Ruth said, they could bring Carl back later. But Matthew didn't like the possibility that they were sending the man home to destroy evidence. Without a warrant, though, what could be done?

While making his way back to Carl's interrogation room, Matthew ran into a frazzled Charli. Matthew had hoped that getting some fresh air and time to herself would take Charli down a notch, but it appeared to have done the opposite. She was wild-eyed and biting her bottom lip, something Matthew had only seen her do in times of extreme stress.

"You all right, Charli?"

"Yes. Why wouldn't I be?" The words shot out of her mouth like darts searching for a target, only adding to Matthew's concern that something was off.

Matthew spent more time with Charli than any other person in his life. Hell, even when he was married, he still saw Charli more than his own wife. That was the nature of the job. Because of this, when Charli was lying to him, he knew it.

"You were at Mami Watu's shop?"

"Yep." She tucked the fraying edges of her pixie cut behind her ears.

"Find anything interesting?"

Charli's face paled. "I-uh, well, nothing concrete. I wanted to know if she had seen any incidents where spells or curses had an impact on the individual. Basically, I was looking to see if there was a possibility the lapses in Carl's memory could be from him convincing himself he was under a curse."

"Huh. There's a thought. Well, the brain is a powerful thing." That could explain why Carl's testimony seemed genuine, despite Dawn Rita claiming he bought a voodoo doll from her.

It didn't explain why Charli's eyes were darting around the room, her face drained of color. Or why her hands slid in and out of her pants pockets, as if she were waiting for something terrible to happen.

Charli had discovered something else at Mami's shop. But what could have bothered her this much? Matthew wanted to ask, but Charli was a stubborn one. If she didn't want Matthew to know, she wasn't going to share.

Charli's eyebrows rose. "Get any further with Carl?"

"Not exactly. And we're not going to get much out of him since Ruth says he needs to be released immediately."

"Oh. That's disappointing." But it wasn't disappointment that Matthew read in Charli's body language. If anything, she seemed grateful to have something to focus on.

"I did find that his son was part of a bar brawl at the Rising Moon. His record didn't pull up much else, though."

Charli rubbed the base of her neck. "Really? That ties Carl in even further. Maybe we need to stop by there again. They didn't know who threatened Jefferson, but I bet they'll know who his son is."

It was great that Charli was acting more like herself,

digging deeper into the investigation. And Matthew needed her skills. Going back to the Rising Moon had not occurred to him. But Charli was right. Carl might not have been known by bargoers, but his son was probably a regular.

"Yeah, let's release Carl and do that right away."

Carl had composed himself somewhat when Charli and Matthew entered the room the older man was waiting in. His bottle of water was emptied, and he looked like a small gust of wind would knock him over.

Though it wasn't good for the investigation if Carl was indeed involved, Matthew empathized with the man. If he was being truthful and had no memory of being involved with Jefferson's death, then he deserved to rest at home after what he'd gone through.

Matthew smiled at Carl, hoping to put the man at ease. "We're going to get you a ride home. I can't say we won't need to call you in for further questions, but for now, head home and rest."

Carl's face drooped with despair. "But we don't have any answers yet. We don't know what happened. I need to know what happened to me, Detectives."

His desperation for answers outweighed his exhaustion, apparently.

Charli stepped forward. "Carl, you've helped us as much as you can for now, but we're not going to have answers overnight. We're doing everything we can to get to the bottom of this. And you'll be the first we call when we know something."

Carl sucked in a deep breath. "Okay. I know you guys must be working hard. It's just jarring to not know what's happened to me."

If Matthew were in Carl's shoes, if he had lost his memory and been drugged by someone, he'd likely react the same way. The urge to learn what had happened would be stronger than any desire to go home.

For all their sakes, maybe more answers were waiting at the Rising Moon.

# 20

A crowd of heads obscured the view of the bar top upon their entry into the Rising Moon. Charli hadn't expected there would be so many people on a Tuesday night, particularly when it had been dead earlier in the day.

It would be a little more difficult to get answers now. They'd have to move through the sea of people to find anyone who could provide information about the case.

"Can you see over these people?" Charli shouted so Matthew could hear.

"Yeah, actually. I think I see Leland at the bar. Follow me."

Matthew's large frame pushed through people with little effort. The sea parted for him, and Charli made sure to stay close behind so the wave wouldn't close in behind Matthew and trap her.

Charli would always be frustrated that she'd been birthed into such a small frame. It was obnoxious to need Matthew's help on tasks like this, but at least he came in handy.

Sure enough, Leland was bartending with a cute redheaded girl who didn't look a day over twenty-two. She had on a lime green crop top that barely covered her breasts and black booty shorts. Evidently, there wasn't much of a dress code at the Rising Moon. The woman leaned over the edge of the bar top flirting with some customers, leaving Leland busy mixing drinks.

So busy, in fact, that it took a moment before he registered that Matthew and Charli were standing right in front of him. He rolled his eyes and planted a hand on his hip.

Leland filled a glass with beer on tap and handed it to a customer before turning back to the detectives. "I thought the point of our earlier conversation was so you wouldn't have to come back here during our busy hours."

"We're in plain clothes, aren't we?" Matthew motioned at his outfit. It was work attire, but nothing that would suggest cops were in the bar. "We won't bother your patrons, I promise. We just want to know if you know of a Micah Perkins."

The bartender wiped up a spill on the countertop. "Micah, yeah, I was working here when he'd come around. Kind of a mess of a kid. Didn't know how to stay out of trouble. Passed away a few years back. What would he have to do with your investigation?"

Matthew declined to answer. "Anything else you can tell us about him?"

Leland never stopped moving, reaching for some empty glasses. "He was an addict, but I'm guessing you know that. One day, when I took my son to a sporting goods store to get new shoes, I ran into him there. He was an employee. Besides that, there's not much else I can tell you. He'd come in here already high, get wasted, and call himself a cab. Didn't regularly interact with any of the other customers or anything. Except when he picked up an attitude, he kept to himself."

His input wasn't much help, but at least they had another witness to Carl's son being present at the bar.

"What do you know about voodoo?" Charli gripped her pen and notebook, glancing up at the bartender. The question was a quick departure from what they were just discussing, and both Leland and Matthew stared at her.

"Uh, not much. Why?"

"Do you know of any voodoo practitioners who frequented the bar?"

Leland wiped down the glasses, setting them under the counter. "If they did, we didn't know about it. Jefferson wouldn't have allowed it. He hated all that voodoo crap. It was personal to him. He would not let voodoo magic into his bar."

That piqued Charli's interest. "Why was voodoo so personal? Did he have another religion he subscribed to instead?"

"No, he wasn't a religious man, but he hated Tany Speers. Never met the woman, but he told me she went after criminals in the city, and he made it his mission to keep anyone who associated with her far away."

*And Tany Speers popped up yet again. But nobody seemed to know where to find the damn woman.*

"Would you happen to know if Tany lives within city limits?" Charli had already run the name when she was at the precinct and found nothing. Perhaps if Tany lived in a different city, Charli could track her down.

"No idea. Like I said, I really only know her through Jefferson." Leland grabbed four shots he had just poured and set them down on the bar top in front of the couple next to Matthew and Charli. His attention was drifting as he turned around to pour a couple of beers from the tap.

They'd likely come to the end of their questioning, anyway. Charli only wanted to ask one more thing.

"Has anyone ever been drugged here at the Rising Moon?"

"Drugged?" Leland raised an eyebrow, appearing downright shocked at the prospect. "As in, against their will?

Didn't happen often that I know of. There was one case of a man who was clearly trying to take advantage of another customer, but he was caught. Serving five years in prison now. Doubt he's of any interest to you guys."

No, he wasn't.

"Thank you for your time." Charli tossed her card on the bar top, not trusting that her previous one had made it any further than the trash can. "We may be in touch."

Leland shook his head, clearly hoping that wouldn't be the case.

All the bodies in the room made the bar hot, even with the AC running. And the kind of people present weren't anyone Charli wanted to linger around. The urge to take off her jacket became overwhelming, something Charli didn't like to do even in the Savannah heat. It held too many important items and documentation. Instead, Charli opted to leave the bar as quickly as possible.

As they exited the building, the sun was fading fast. They had maybe twenty more minutes of daylight left, and it appeared they'd exhausted their current sources of information.

"What do you say we call it a day? We had a long night. Probably best if we head home and get some rest." Matthew thrust his arms up for an extended stretch.

Charli yawned at the idea of getting back home. "Not a bad idea. We should look at this with fresh eyes tomorrow."

And maybe with a little sleep, Charli could shake off the day's strange events and get a break in the case.

# 21

Tall grass itched at my calves, though I didn't mind. There was something soothing about these swampy marshes that called to me, making me feel at home.

If Old Burn Road wasn't full of addicts and lunatics, perhaps I would consider moving out here. I was more in touch with nature in this area than I'd ever been in the city. In the night sky, the stars twinkled so much brighter than they did back home. I was staring into a sea of fireballs, and they all took turns winking at me. A symphony of frogs and crickets accompanied the brilliant light show.

But I was allowing myself to become far too distracted. I'd come here for a reason. I had a purpose to fulfill. The heavy breathing of the monster behind me was a reminder. I released a deep sigh, the weight of what was about to happen heavy upon my spirit.

"You must calm yourself." I kept my voice low as I spoke to the beast. "We will have our time. It is near."

As I walked, I steadied my own breathing, willing myself the mental and physical strength to do what had to be done tonight. My recent visit with a medical doctor crept into my mind, but I pushed it aside. There was no time for that now, and I knew Papa Legba would grant me the strength I needed.

I crept through the edge of the grass, hoping to get a view inside the home, if it could be called such a thing. The dwelling seemed more like a temporary shelter that the big bad wolf could huff and puff and send it tumbling down.

That was exactly what was about to happen, though. I was the big bad wolf. She was the careless pig inside. *And what did wolves do to careless pigs? Well...they did what wild animals did, of course.*

The witch deserved every bit of my wrath coming toward her. She had not earned the right to call herself a voodoo priestess. What positive thing had she done for her community? Nothing would be an understatement. She'd done worse than nothing.

While I was trying to get addicts to see the light, she was scamming them in their lowest moments. Voodoo was just a financial practice to her, and I had been willing to ignore that. But I could no longer allow her practices to continue, not if she could put my identity at risk.

Yet still, the seriousness of the deed I would soon commit weighed upon my soul. At war with myself, I wrestled with the idea of committing such a heinous act. *Was this the only way? Should I go through with my plan?* Doubts swirled around in my mind.

But the witch had to be silenced. I'd prayed to Papa Legba, and he'd granted me his permission to cast this wretched soul into his kingdom. He released me of my guilt at that moment. Her death was the right thing for this world.

And I wouldn't be killing her anyway, not really. The monster would. That was what he was here for.

He stalked behind me like a shadow, despite towering over my body. His great height was of no consequence, though. After nightfall, he blended in with the dark swamps surrounding us. The witch would never see us coming.

I edged along the property until I spotted a window on the right side of the little shack. There she was, leaning over the table. The witch was setting the table and lighting candles. Was she expecting company tonight?

*The company had just arrived.*

"We need to move now. Someone may be arriving." My eyes darted to the shadow behind me.

The only response I received was a grunt, but I had no doubt it was an affirmation of my plan.

"Stay out of sight, and don't go inside until after I leave." I didn't want to alert her to my plan, not at first.

Taking care not to bump anything in the dark, I moved onto the patio and knocked on the door, leaning against the wall so she wouldn't get a chance to see me before I barged in.

"Hey, you're early! Crawdads won't be ready for a while." The door muffled her voice, but thanks to the poor insulation, I could still hear well enough.

I sucked in a deep breath as the doorknob began to jiggle. Adrenaline coursed through my body, coupled with righteous indignation. As soon as the draft from the open door hit my cheek, I pounced on my prey.

*Wham!*

With all the power within me, I rammed into her, knocking her to the floor. The witch crumpled in a heap, her left arm pinned under the weight of her body.

She shrieked like a stuck pig. Beads of sweat glistened on her face as she writhed on the floor in pain. She struggled to roll onto her back, cradling the arm that had broken her fall.

Releasing her now limp arm, she used her uninjured limb to hoist herself off the floor. She shuffled to her feet with a grunt, her right one sliding out from under her at first. With labored breaths, she swerved around to discover her assailant.

Shock mingled with fury on her face.

"*You*? What are *you* doing here?"

"Don't you know? Or are you really that slow?"

"It was you, huh? I thought it might be." I smelled the fear radiating from her skin, betraying her calm veneer.

"I know what you thought. That's why I'm here. To make sure you don't go spilling those thoughts."

The brave façade slipped away. "Of course, I'm not gonna! Who do you think I am? You know better than that."

"I think you're a shady, slimy little witch who has always gotten herself into trouble, and you will not take me down with you."

Her eyes drifted to the shadow lurking beyond the open door. In slow motion, the monster trudged into the dwelling, closing the door behind him. His face twitched, a sadistic smile playing at his lips.

A single tear spilled from the corner of the witch's eye and trickled down her cheek. "Don't do this. I'll leave you be, Ta—"

*Smack!*

The slap stung my palm with the effort. My body was still weak from my collision with the witch, and I failed to still the trembling of my hands. "Don't. Ever. Say. My. Name."

The floodgates opened wide, her tears falling in torrents. She buried her face in her hands. "I w-won't. I swear."

"You won't have to remember anything at all when he's finished."

I snapped my fingers, and the monster descended, tackling her to the floor.

I hurried outside, my soul satisfied that the monster would do my bidding. Hollow screams carried out of the house and into the swampland, but I wasn't worried about that.

Feeling no guilt, I raised my hands in praise to Papa Legba for easing my path to righteousness this glorious night.

## 22

*The golden bell above the front door rang out as Charli pulled it open to enter Mami Watu's shop. Nobody was in the front, but Charli's name echoed from the back room.*

*"I've been waiting for you, Detective." Mami Watu's voice rang off the white walls of the empty shop.*

*Every nerve in Charli's body willed her to walk out the door. She didn't need to be here. It was time to leave.*

*But her feet continued moving forward until she reached the back room where Mami Watu sat with a large kettle of boiling water. An ornate blue teacup sat perched on the empty chair across from the voodoo priestess.*

*"Would you like another cup of tea?" Mami's hollow cheekbones jutted out from her face.*

*"No." But Charli sat down anyway. Her hands gripped the arms of the chair, nails digging so deep into the fabric she worried it would tear.*

*What was she doing here? She wanted to leave. It was like her hands were glued to the chair to keep her from escaping. Her body weighed her down like a hundred pounds of rocks tossed into the velvet seat. Charli couldn't have risen even if she tried.*

*Her heart raced in her chest, and she gasped for air. "Why are you doing this? And how are you doing it? I don't want to be here."*

*"Then why did you come?" With an innocent tilt of her head, Mami's curious eyes seemed to penetrate Charli's soul.*

*"I...I don't know." Charli barely remembered the trip, actually. Why had she made the drive? Why did she decide to walk through the door? It was all a blur.*

*Somehow, the voodoo priestess was responsible for this. She'd cast a spell on Charli that forced her to come back to the shop.*

*Why would she do that, though? What did she have to gain from Charli returning?*

*"You brought me here."*

*"Prove it." The older woman's smile vanished. Her flaming eyes shot daggers at Charli.*

*"Why do you want me here?" Charli's voice roared loud enough for the entire neighborhood to hear. And she hoped they would. Someone had to come save her.*

*Her mind drifted to her partner. Was he aware she was here? Charli would have told him if she planned to go back to Mami Watu's shop. Matthew would come for her, surely.*

*"He won't save you." Mami read her mind. "And why should he? Do you think you deserve it after you didn't save...her?"*

*Her pulse began to pound in her throat. "Who...who are you talking about?"*

*But she knew. And she shouldn't have asked. Now the priestess had another excuse to speak her name, and Charli didn't want to hear it.*

*"Madeline, of course."*

*Warm, salty tears dripped down Charli's cheeks like drops of rain racing down a car window. "Don't use her against me."*

*Mami Watu's face softened once again. Her voice oozed empathy. "Oh, we don't need to go there right now. Let's get back to what you came here for. How about another reading?"*

*The word* no *danced in Charli's head, but it wouldn't come out. "Okay."*

*Mami didn't use her palm this time. Instead, she grabbed a large crystal ball that sat on a wood platform. It had to be eight inches in diameter. The fluorescent light from above made the clear ball glow.*

*"Now, where were we? Oh, yes...Madeline." Mami Watu rubbed the crystal ball.*

*Charli's eyes were glued to the globe as a swirling image began to form inside the sphere. It was Charli's shoe. Not the one she was wearing now, but one she had on the day Madeline disappeared. A white, scuffed up Converse. Her left shoelace was untied, and Charli kneeled down to tie it.*

*Her gaze remained on the shoe until a screech beckoned her vision upward. A shadowy figure yanked away her best friend.*

*"Charli, help me!"*

*Charli tried, running as fast as she could, but her feet remained planted on the wet grass. She was on an invisible treadmill, cursed to go no farther than where she already stood.*

*"I can't! I'm trying, but I can't!" Charli reached out as the figure continued to drag Madeline away.*

*"But if you tried harder, you could! If you really loved me, you could! How can you fail me now?"*

*Rocks dropped into Charli's stomach. Everything she'd eaten that day threatened to spew out. Madeline was right. She was failing her.*

*"I don't want to! I want to help you! I want to help so bad!"*

*"But you never will! You're going to fail me...and so many victims after me!"*

*The shadowy figure tossed Madeline into the back of the van before she could get out another word. Charli's cry forced a flock of crows nearby to scatter toward the sky. But no matter how she screamed, the van wouldn't come back.*

*But the image was no longer visible. Charli raised her attention from the glass. Mami Watu still gazed into the ball. Sadness leaked from the corners of the older woman's eyes.*

*"What a disappointment you were to her."*

*Charli's voice caught in her throat. She couldn't muster a defense.*

*"And she isn't the only one you're going to fail. How many other people already died because you couldn't get to them fast enough?"*

*The tears didn't trickle anymore. They flowed like a waterfall. "I'm so sorry."*

*"But sorry won't save them, and it won't save your next victim, either. Better wake up and find her."*

Charli's eyes fluttered open after little more than an hour of sleep. It wasn't even near midnight yet. She'd gone to bed early, but it seemed an impossible feat to rest an entire night. A chill racked her body as her mind filtered images from her most recent dream.

It had been a mistake to agree to that free reading. It had seemed harmless, but Charli could not focus on the case while she was stuck on what Mami Watu had said. What more could she know about Madeline?

Dwelling on it was foolish, Charli was aware, but she could not shake the questions that kept repeating in the back of her mind. *Could Mami Watu provide insight into what had happened that day? Was there a chance she could lead Charli to who had taken her?*

A week ago, Charli would've thought it impossible that she'd ever consider the possibility that voodoo magic could actually work.

The alarm clock read nine forty-five in bright red numbers. It would be best if Charli rolled over and tried to get more rest, but her mind was completely awake. If she couldn't go back to bed, maybe the best thing to do was try to bring herself back to reality.

She grabbed her phone on her nightstand and searched

for *The Serpent and the Rainbow* once more. It wasn't as if Charli didn't know the story already, but perhaps seeing the plot play out again would remind her that voodoo was a parlor trick. If magic appeared real, there was a reasonable explanation behind it.

Reading the story once more actually helped calm Charli's racing mind. When she finished, she looked through the unread text messages she'd been neglecting. While most of them were notifications about bills on automatic withdrawal, she also received a text from her father.

*Tried to call, but guess I missed ya. You're probably working hard on a new case. Just wanted to let you know I stopped by the doctor and got a clean bill of health. Thought you might be happy to hear that. Give me a ring when you're not too busy. Hope you're taking care of yourself.*

Normally, any mention of Charli's work came with a lecture about her career choice. But it was nice that he said nothing except how she must be working hard.

*I am glad to hear that, Dad. And I am working on a new case. It's a lot, but I'll give you a call this weekend to catch up. Sending you my love.*

It was formal for a text message, but her dad used texts more like conventional letters.

Charli had been too busy to think about her father, but now that he'd reached out, she realized how much she'd needed to hear from him. In one day, she'd had to deal with the hospital reminding her of her mother's death, Madeline's kidnapping, and snapping at a witness for no reason. It was nice for a parental figure to send some well wishes.

No matter how old Charli got or how independent she tried to seem, there was always that inner child craving the comfort of her parents. Maybe that was how it was for everyone.

After reading her dad's text, Charli might actually be

ready to fall back asleep. But as soon as she set her phone down, it started ringing. She sighed. Ruth's name sent her sitting up with a jolt.

"Detective Cross."

"Good, you're awake. I need you to get in touch with Matthew. Both of you need to meet down at Old Burn Road."

*What the hell had happened now?*

"Why?"

"There's been another voodoo-related murder. I'm staring at a picture of a doll that looks exactly like the one held in Jefferson and Carl's hands. Although this time, the doll's covered in blood."

Charli's heart sank as her dream echoed in her mind. Old Burn Road. She had a pretty good guess as to who it was, but she had to ask.

"And who is the victim?"

Charli closed her eyes as Ruth confirmed her fear. "Dawn Rita Molette."

## 23

Matthew rubbed his eyes, blinking hard. He was glad his partner was driving, though Charli looked as tired as he felt.

"I shouldn't have done that." Charli's voice held an edge of guilt and shame. "I shouldn't have snapped at her."

Matthew was still half asleep, but Charli was wide awake as she continued to berate herself. He wanted to reach over and pat her arm and tell her that she had nothing to feel guilty about. But he knew she didn't want to be comforted. He knew her well enough to realize that much.

He hardened his voice. "Charli, you snapping a few words didn't kill this woman. Try to focus on the street." It was dark out on Old Burn Road. There weren't enough streetlights to illuminate the way.

Charli kept her eyes on the road, straining to see beyond the glow of the headlights. "I know it didn't, but still. I'm supposed to be a professional, and I made an assumption."

"It happens to the best of us. It's the stress of the job." Matthew had had his fair share of emotional outbursts.

"Not to me, it doesn't." Charli clenched her jaw.

Matthew sighed, rubbing his face again. "Maybe that's part of the problem. You put yourself up on this pedestal of perfection so that the second you fall off it, everything splits into pieces. Don't you think that could be why you're so stressed right now?"

Charli didn't answer but pointed to the cop car in front of them. "Here we are."

Even with the headlights of both cars, Dawn Rita's home was creepy as hell at night. The headlights only made the scene more sinister. The opened front door was lit up, and Matthew could only imagine what they would find inside.

"Ruth said the scene was bloody?" Matthew's stomach was churning already.

"A total gore fest, apparently."

Matthew hated these crime scenes the most. It was hard enough to see a dead body that wasn't dripping in blood. And Ruth didn't often go out of her way to describe a crime scene as gory. If she felt she needed to mention blood, it was going to be bad.

He sighed. "Let's get this over with."

The officer, Theodore West, was already at their door when they got out, the logbook in hand.

"Have you two been briefed?" He glanced at the detectives as Charli and Matthew signed in.

"Only the most basic information." Charli slammed her car door shut.

"She was found by a friend, a local man named Freddy Reed. Can't tell if he was a romantic partner or just a buddy because he doesn't seem to want to say. But every week, he and Dawn would drink and eat crawdads together, just to chew the fat."

"Were they going to do that tonight?" If they weren't, it would make no sense why Freddy would find her.

"That's what he says, and the story checks out. There

were crawdads boiling on the stove. He didn't see anyone come or go."

"He still here?" Matthew swiveled his head around to peer into the dark shadows.

"I've got him sitting in my car."

"Let's check out the scene first." Charli motioned toward the house wrapped in bright yellow crime scene tape. "A look around might help us formulate any questions we want to ask him."

The detectives pulled on booties over their shoes before stepping into the house.

Dread zipped through Matthew's veins as he stepped onto the same porch he'd drunk sweet tea on just hours earlier. The poor woman had offered the detectives cake. She seemed off, sure, but Dawn had been compliant with the investigation. Their recent close contact with her made it even more disturbing to walk into her home and see blood doused all over the floor.

The blood was the least unsightly factor in the scene, though. In the living room, Dawn Rita's body had been chopped apart, and the pieces reassembled as each body part was pinned to the wall. Looking like a gory voodoo doll, at least a dozen nails held her upright. A doll had been nailed through her right palm, giving the perception that Dawn was holding the creepy looking toy. The horror in Dawn's open eyes infiltrated Matthew's soul.

The forensics team arrived and began taking photographs. As soon as Matthew viewed the body, he was eager to exit the house. While it was necessary for him to inspect the crime scene, there was nobody here for Matthew to question. If the medical examiner had been present, Matthew would've forced himself to stay and get all the gritty details. But since the 911 call occurred less than an hour ago, he supposed the M.E. likely needed time to get out to Old Burn. And in this case, Matthew didn't want to stick around for much longer.

"The M.E. isn't here yet. Maybe it's best we go interview Freddy while we wait for him."

Matthew used meeting Freddy and getting his impression of what happened as an excuse to get out of the house. If Charli was aware of this, she pretended not to be.

"Sounds good to me." Charli moved in front of him, swinging her left leg and then her right over the crime scene tape.

Being considerably taller than his partner, Matthew didn't have to put as much effort into the process, stepping over the tape with only a slight rise to his normal stride. After taking the protective coverings off their shoes, they moved to the car where Freddy waited.

"Hi, Freddy. I'm Detective Cross, and this is Detective Church. Can you tell me about what you witnessed here tonight?"

Freddy buried his face in his hands. "I was gonna spend my night with Dawn, eating crawdads and sharin' in a bottle. But when I got here, the door was hanging wide, and she was up on the wall. I don't know nothin' more than that."

Matthew laid a hand against the police cruiser. "What time did you arrive tonight?"

Freddy wiped his face on his sleeve. "I was a little late to our dinner. Showed up around twenty minutes after nine."

Charli peered through the window at their witness. "And what was Dawn to you?"

"Dawn's my friend. It's hard out here on Ol' Burn. We gotta find people we can rely on. Dawn and I liked to spend time together."

"Were you aware of Dawn's connection to voodoo?" Matthew wanted to make sure they followed every possible voodoo connection.

Lifting his head, Freddy gave no indication that her practice of voodoo bothered him. "Yeah, I know. She was known for it 'round here."

"Are you a believer yourself?" Charli's voice was soft.

Freddy reached up and pushed his dark curls out of his eyes. "Sure am."

He'd said the words with so much confidence and conviction, Matthew hoped Freddy might turn into a good source of information regarding other local voodoo practitioners. "Can you walk us through your night prior to arriving at Dawn's?" Matthew wanted to ask about Tany Speers and Mami Watu, but he first had to establish an alibi.

"I was with my daughter at her house. That was why I was late. We were talkin' about her latest job. She's had troubles with her car and arrivin' on time. It's hard when you live out in the sticks. But I realized the time and told her I had to go eat with Dawn. When I came and saw her door wide open, I walked in real slow. That's when…" Freddy's voice cracked, and a sob racked his body.

Charli pulled a tissue from her pocket and handed it to the man, giving him a few moments to compose himself. "I know it's difficult, but we need to know exactly what you saw tonight."

Freddy blew his nose. "Her body was mangled up. Someone did her in real bad. I called 911 right away. That's all that happened."

Charli opened her notepad. "Do you know anyone who'd want to harm Dawn?"

Freddy scrubbed a hand over his face, blinking his dark eyes several times. "No, nobody."

Matthew drew in a deep breath. "Freddy, are you familiar with any other voodoo practitioners?"

"Practitioners?"

"You know, anyone who engages with voodoo magic."

"Oh, I see, you mean like Tany Speers and Mami Watu." Another shudder racked through him. "They're the only ones I know of. Only ever met Mami Watu. She's a lovely woman. She comes out and brings toys to the children out here. Dawn bought stuff from her shop too."

Freddy talked as if Dawn and Mami were friends. But from speaking to their latest victim, she hadn't seemed to trust the woman.

"And what about Tany?"

His face drained of emotion, but his eyes darted around as if he was worried the woman might appear next to him. "Tany is a scary soul. She's not like Dawn or Mami Watu. She punishes people. Even for things they can't control, like drinkin'. I don't like drinkin', Detective. But it's hard to stop. Tany Speers would punish someone like me."

"But you've never met her, right? Do you know where she lives?" The frustration was building in Matthew's chest. *Why didn't anyone ever have concrete information about Tany Speers?*

"I only know rumors. Never seen her. Don't know where she lives." He wiped his nose again. "Don't want to know."

"Would she punish someone like Dawn?"

Freddy paused on this thought. "She could punish anyone. I don't know what Dawn would've done, but Tany could've punished her."

"Why don't you think Mami Watu would have done anything to harm Dawn?" Although Freddy had made it clear how he viewed Mami, Matthew couldn't ignore the two women's obvious dislike for each other. And Mami obviously had her hand in voodoo.

"Because Mami Watu is good. Some people look down on her like Dawn did. They call Mami a witch. But she's never done harm to nobody that I know of. And being friends with Dawn taught me there are lotsa good witches out there. Dawn was so sweet." Freddy pressed a hand to his chest, and he gasped so loud Matthew worried that he might be having a heart attack, but he went on, shaking his head. "Why would anyone do this to her?"

"I don't know, Freddy. But we're going to find out."

After getting information regarding an alibi, Matthew proceeded to release Freddy for the night on the condition that he be available to talk in the future if they sought him out. There was no sense in continuing to torture this man tonight.

"Do you need an escort home, Freddy?" After what he'd been through, Matthew thought he might need someone to give him a sense of safety.

"No, sir. I only live a block away. I can walk."

When Freddy was out of earshot, Charli let out a loud groan.

"Dammit!" She kicked a nearby patch of weeds. "Why does everyone know of this Tany woman, but nobody knows where to find her? I get now what people mean when they say she's a legend. Is she even real?"

"Mami Watu seemed to know her, even if they hadn't spoken in several years. If she's responsible for this, we'll find her, eventually. But I think we need to entertain the idea that Carl had a part in this."

Charli leaned against the cop car. "Yeah, that's where my mind was heading too. We release him after mentioning that Dawn claimed to have sold him a voodoo doll, and she's murdered the same night? It's suspicious."

Although Matthew was open to the possibility, he hoped this wasn't the case. Because if it was, Matthew and Charli had gotten Dawn killed by mentioning her to Carl.

"While forensics finish up, maybe we should go see what Carl is up to."

"Call a squad car over there now to check in on him.

Someone will be closer than we are, and if he's leaving this scene, we might be able to catch him in the act."

"Good call." Matthew did as Charli suggested.

Of course, if Carl was guilty, then they needed to catch him in the act. If he was in his house and refused to answer the door, there was little they could do to enter. Matthew was going to discuss this with Charli, but when he saw her face, her eyes were fixated on something in the distance.

"What is it?"

"Give me your flashlight." Charli reached toward Matthew but kept her gaze focused on whatever had caught her eye.

The light wasn't on Matthew's person but in the car. He walked over to the cruiser, leaving her where she stood. Somehow, though she might as well have been a statue still standing in that spot, when Matthew put the flashlight in her hand, she barely shifted and turned the power on.

"Do you see that?" Charli pointed the bright light toward the corner of the backyard.

He peered in that direction, straining his eyes. "No, see what?"

Without warning, a shadow moved across the circle of light. Charli bolted, flashlight still in hand. Matthew darted after his partner.

There was definitely a person trying to make their escape, and though he couldn't be sure, Matthew thought the fleeing person was a man. Every few seconds, the flashlight exposed them as they ran through the swamps.

Whoever it was did not know the area well. Matthew didn't think the man was a neighbor because the direction he was running would take him straight to the water. He'd be trapped.

*Unless he had a boat?*

*Shit!*

Matthew didn't know how long he could keep pace with Charli. For one thing, he was out of shape and hadn't been for a run in who knew how long. And he seemed to have a lot less energy than his partner. Every footfall in the grass was heavy. If he wasn't careful, he'd get tangled in the weeds and fall.

"Freeze!" Though she was tiny, Charli's command voice was not.

The figure didn't listen at first. But when his feet fell into a muddy marsh, he was stopped in his tracks.

Charli grabbed the runner by the shirt collar and flipped him over before flashing the light in his face.

Matthew was right. It was a man.

"Mr. De Bassio?"

# 24

Was Charli losing her edge?

Never once had she considered that Cedric De Bassio could be a suspect. Carl, Dawn Rita, and even Mami Watu had been front and center in Charli's mind. And yet, she'd never considered Cedric to be anything other than a witness.

In retrospect, that was stupid. Cedric had access to the cemetery in a way nobody else did. Both of their victims were found in the cemetery. Sure, the groundskeeper had put on a big show about how afraid he was of voodoo, but that could have been fake.

This case continued to throw Charli for a loop. She was tired of not being on her A-game. That was going to end now. She'd use this moment with Cedric to get the information she desperately needed.

Cedric thrust his hands up in the air. "Please don't shoot." The terror on his face could be the result of him being a talented actor, just as the sweat dripping down his face could be due to the heat. But the gray tinge to his dark skin wasn't something easily faked. He was scared, and his fear was deep-rooted.

"We aren't going to shoot you, but you need to stay right here." Charli was breathing hard from the chase and the rush of adrenaline still swirling through her system. "You know it's illegal to run from an officer of the law that way, right?" She began patting him down, pissed at herself for not having tucked a pair of handcuffs into her pocket. "You don't have anything sharp on you that will hurt me, do you?"

Cedric turned his head to the left, glancing over his shoulder at Charli. His right cheek was pressed to the ground. "N-no."

After she'd searched his pockets and completed the pat down, she and Matthew pulled him to his feet. With a hand on each of their captive's arms, they escorted him back to the front of the house. It wasn't easy. The mud suctioned to Charli's boots with every step.

Sweat streamed down Cedric's cheeks and dripped from his chin. "Am I u-under arrest?"

"Not yet." Matthew turned Cedric until his back pressed against a nearby patrol car. "Answer our questions, and we'll see if it stays that way."

Charli searched his face. "Why did you run?"

Cedric's hands were still trembling badly, and he nearly smacked himself in the face when he attempted to wipe the sweat from his brow. "I didn't know you were the cops at first. I was worried you were criminals yourselves. And once I figured it out, I got scared about how it looked and just kept going. But I ain't run like that in years. I'm too old for this."

In the darkness of the swamps, there was only the light from the house to illuminate Cedric's face. The angles of his features cast eerie shadows, giving him an otherworldly impression. Charli tried to push away the discomfort this caused. *Why did everything about this case have to be so creepy?*

Matthew's hand was on his gun. "Cedric, what are you doing here?"

The whites of his eyes grew larger. "I don't even know!"

"Do you live on Old Burn Road, Cedric?" This was key information. Charli expected that the man lived closer to the cemetery, and if that was the case, there was no reason for him to be out here so late at night.

Cedric's chest heaved with each ragged breath he drew. "No. I live in Savannah. I drove out here, but I got turned around. I was parked a few houses down, and I was wandering around to find Dawn Rita's house. I thought maybe I'd found the right place, but then I was even more confused when so many people were coming in and out of it."

"Tell us everything you did before coming out to Old Burn tonight." Matthew kept his gaze on the groundskeeper.

Cedric leaned forward, resting his palms on his thighs. Charli could tell he was having a hard time catching his breath. "I wasn't doing anything before coming here. I worked my shift at the cemetery, and then I went home to go to bed, but I couldn't fall asleep. I haven't been able to sleep for days. I was growing desperate, so I drove out here to visit Dawn Rita."

So, he intended to see Dawn Rita? But that made no sense. If Freddy had been telling the truth, then Dawn Rita already had plans tonight. And it was a benign thing for Freddy to lie about. He claimed he and Dawn had dinner fairly regularly, which would be easy enough for Charli to confirm.

"Was Dawn expecting you, Cedric?" Charli was careful not to let the words come across as accusatory.

"No, I don't know her number. I couldn't tell her I was coming. I just..." Cedric let out a long breath.

Charli pinned him with her gaze. "You just what?"

The groundskeeper straightened up, his breathing beginning to slow. "I needed help. I just needed help." His voice was a mix of desperation and confusion. "How did I get here?"

"I don't know. You tell me." Charli had mud on her pants and was starting to feel a chill. They'd need to go back to the car soon, but it was best to question Cedric now while he was frazzled. Honest answers could be attained from a shaken individual.

Cedric threw his arms in the air, gesturing wildly. Charli was afraid he'd hyperventilate. "You don't know what it's been like. I told y'all that I don't mess with voodoo! But now it's messed with me! Ever since I found that body, I haven't been right. And the nightmares..."

The conversation was like conversing with a dementia patient. There were moments of lucidity when Cedric explained his thought process, and then he'd cease speaking. Was this normal behavior for Cedric? He was only in his sixties, so while not likely, it was possible.

"Nightmares about what?" Charli had to keep him on track.

Cedric covered his face with his hands, his fingers glistening with sweat from his cheeks when he finally lowered them. "The body! And so many other bodies! I can't take it anymore. I thought Dawn could take this curse from me. She's powerful. I've heard people say so. Only one stronger is Tany, but ain't nobody can tell me how to get to her. I need Dawn."

Although, with careful consideration, a perpetrator could control their language, it was worth noting that Cedric was speaking about Dawn in the present tense.

"You're not going to be able to speak to Dawn tonight." Matthew's tone was cool but discerning.

For whatever reason, this sent Cedric into an absolute

frenzy. "No! No! I came all this way for Dawn. You go get me Dawn. She's going to save me! I need her to save me!"

Perhaps Mami Watu had been onto something when she said Dawn Rita took advantage of mentally unstable individuals. Cedric was obviously not in his right mind. If Dawn were still alive, would she have charged him for her help?

Though even if she did, was that really so bad? If Cedric convinced himself he was actually cured afterward, perhaps it was worth it. Or, in the strangest possibility, maybe Dawn actually could help with his delusions.

"Cedric, Dawn is dead. She was killed this evening." The information was Charli's way of garnering one last big reaction before they had to drag him to the car.

"What?" Cedric stilled. "No, that can't be. She's the only one who can save me."

Matthew took a few steps back and lowered his voice. "I'm going to call a paramedic. He might just be tired, but let's clear him of any medical condition and then get him down to the station for questioning."

Charli nodded but didn't answer. She was too busy observing Cedric for any additional signs of agitation. But all she could gather from him was a stare of despair.

Charli wasn't hopeful that anything was going to come from questioning Cedric. She was going to do so because an interview was the only way to gather information and rule him out, but if he was being honest that he only came out here for a remedy, then his information was of little use.

Charli thrust her hands into her pockets. Every time they got close to finding out the truth, they took ten steps backward.

# 25

Matthew peeked into the viewing room to find Charli with her gaze pinned on De Bassio on the other side of the glass. Although she was focused, she stifled a yawn. He stepped into the room, but she wasn't aware of his presence until the door shut with a soft click.

She jumped, whirling to face him, then relaxed against the window when she realized it was him. "Find anything?"

He was tempted to tease her about being so jumpy but decided that he preferred to keep his balls on the outside of his body. "Nothing. De Bassio has a clean record. The only mention of him in any criminal documents is from breaking up fights and reporting vandals at the cemetery. I talked to the officer we sent to check in on Carl Jenkins too. He said nobody's answered his knocks. How's Cedric doing?"

She faced the glass again, studying the man on the other side. "He's definitely worked up, but that could be from anything. A lot of people are nervous about being dragged down to the precinct for questioning. We won't know more until we start interviewing him."

"Then let's get to it." Back in the hallway, Matthew

opened the door to the interrogation room, letting Charli walk in first.

Before they could even sit down, Cedric was sputtering out an explanation. "You don't understand, okay? I don't have no part of this. Only went to Dawn's to get answers!"

The chair's metal legs screeched against the floor as Charli pulled it back to take a seat. "Answers about what?"

"About these damn dreams." Cedric raised his hands, gesturing wildly. It made Matthew want to cuff him again. "I've been haunted since I saw that body."

His words weren't funny in a laugh-out-loud kind of way, but there was an ironic humor to all of this. Cedric dealt with dead bodies for a living. He worked in a cemetery. It was a place most people wouldn't venture into for a thousand bucks. But this was Cedric's life work. And this one body had him terrified? The sudden fear made his story a little suspect.

"Cedric, if you were going to be haunted, don't you think it would've happened by now?" Matthew spread his hands in a silent question. "How many funerals have you been witness to? You've seen a multitude of bodies lowered into the ground."

"It ain't the same." Sweat rolled down their suspect's temples. His almond-colored eyes shifted around the room. "Those bodies came to my cemetery to rest. A body can have peace, or it can have a vengeance. The second I saw that damn doll, I knew that vengeance was comin' for me too. And it has." He began to rock in his chair. "I can't sleep or eat."

The heavy bags under his eyes suggested he was speaking the truth about that.

"You've got to understand our confusion here, Cedric." Matthew lifted a finger, ready to count off all the ways he was about to paint a picture of this man's guilt. "We find you walking around the swamps late at night." A second finger went up. "The house was surrounded with crime scene tape, and yet you lingered." A third joined in. "Then, when you saw us, you sprinted away. You see how suspicious this is?"

"I know." Cedric began rocking harder. "Of course, I know how it looks. But I only wanted help. Honest."

"Why didn't you park right in front of Dawn's house?" Charli raised an eyebrow. "You parked down the street and walked to her. That's pretty suspicious too. It seems like you didn't want to be seen near Dawn's place."

"I didn't, but not for the reasons you're claimin'." Cedric leaned forward, peering at Charli. "Look, I know what Old Burn Road is. People already think I'm a weirdo for working in the cemetery. I don't want anyone thinkin' I believe in voodoo too. That's a bad look for me."

Matthew just stared at the man because it was pretty clear that Cedric did believe in voodoo. If he didn't, there was no reason for him to go to Dawn's.

Matthew was tired of the double-talk and decided to put a little more pressure on. "What *do* you believe?"

"I believe you don't mess with voodoo." Cedric ran a shaky hand down his button-up shirt. "You don't touch the spirit world. And I kept myself safe in the decades I worked at the cemetery because I have respect for that other world." He lowered his voice, his eyes rolling toward the heavens. "Now, I feel like this has been forced on me. People say that Dawn was the real deal, and I thought maybe she could take," he slammed a fist into his chest, "this thing from me."

The room was silent for a long moment, and goose bumps raised on Matthew's arms. He wasn't afraid, not really. But he was certainly picking up the fear from the other man.

Charli tapped her pen against her notepad. "Any other real deal voodoo practitioners you know about?"

A drop of sweat dripped from Cedric's chin as he took in a deep breath. "Mami Watu was my first stop, but her shop was closed this late, and I couldn't take one more night of this." He scoffed and crossed himself. "And I ain't about to try to hunt down Tany. People say she keeps her location locked up tight these days."

Charli glanced at Matthew, her eyes bright in anticipation. "What do you know about both Tany and Mami?"

Cedric crossed himself again. "I been hearing rumors for years. A lot of people into voodoo show up at the cemetery, ready to use it as a place to do their creepy curses. I know Tany is even more powerful than Mami Watu. Tany taught Mami all she knows."

Charli gave Matthew another sideways glance. "Tany Speers was Mami Watu's teacher?"

It was as much a question to Matthew as to Cedric. Matthew could read his partner's mind. *Why didn't Mami tell us this herself?* She had mentioned knowing Tany, but not that Tany had acted as her mentor.

And if Tany was indeed Mami Watu's teacher, it didn't make Mami look too good. Tany Speers had been painted as a criminal, not the kind of character a respectable practitioner would want to study under.

But that could all be nothing more than a rumor. And even if it was true, who knew what kind of person Tany Speers was a decade ago? She may not have operated under the reputation she had now.

"Can you think of any other details?" Charli scribbled some additional notes.

"No. Like I said, I tried to keep far from all that mess. Never even met either of them. Never met Dawn, neither."

Matthew's fingers rapped against the cold metal table, and he decided now would be a good time to back off and try some alternative theories to see if they could pry additional information out of the man. "Okay, fine, Cedric. Let's say you had no part in this crime. Did you happen to see anyone come or go from Dawn's home?"

Cedric's eyes drifted to the table. "Just the police. You were already there when I started walkin' up. Should've left right then and there." He paused, his hand coming up to cross himself again. "But something came over me."

"What does that mean? What came over you?" Matthew wanted to shake the man but delivered his questions calmly. He had to know this didn't sound like a credible explanation.

"I don't know, Detective." Cedric met Matthew's gaze, his irises surrounded by a fiery red where the whites should have been. "Like I said, I haven't been gettin' much sleep. Suddenly, I got all foggy. Everything was confusing. I don't think I snapped out of it 'til you started chasing me, maybe not even then."

The more they talked, the calmer Cedric seemed to become. It was as though piecing the story together with the detectives made the night easier to understand.

But for Matthew, the explanation only left more questions. Questions that, unfortunately, it didn't seem Cedric would help with.

"Can I go home now?" Cedric rubbed his bloodshot eyes.

"Not yet. Not until we can confirm your alibi. You were still the only person at the crime scene, and you ran from us. Resisted arrest." Matthew wasn't aiming to be accusatory. There was no need to berate him any further, but it would be reckless to allow him to walk away.

"That's fine. You'll see soon enough. I ain't had anything to do with this. Check the security cameras at my apartment. They'll show you when I left. In the meantime, I'm gonna get some sleep in a place that I know is safe." Cedric folded his arms on the table and rested his head.

This triggered another yawn from Charli, and she motioned to the door of the observation room.

"I can get a call out to his apartment manager." Matthew let the door fall closed behind him. "But if the cameras can indeed clear him, what's next?"

Charli bit her lip. "We know it's unlikely we're going to hear from Carl Perkins tonight. Do we have anyone set up outside his apartment?"

"Same officer who knocked on the door is staking it out. If he comes or goes, we'll know. And he's ready to detain him the second he sees him."

"Then Mami Watu is our next bet. The fact that she misled us about her relationship with Tany is a big red flag. Maybe she's not as clean-cut as she wants everyone to think."

Matthew had the same idea. "And if she was that close to Tany, she has to know something about her real name. Surely, she has identifying information. We absolutely have to track down Tany Speers. Anytime we so much as mention voodoo, that name comes up."

Charli glanced at her watch, and Matthew did the same. It was seven minutes past midnight. A little late for a visit, but…he could tell by the look in Charli's eyes, she didn't care.

"To Mami Watu's it is. If she truly wants to 'help,'" Charli air quoted the word, "she won't mind." Charli's words were determined, but her face was another story. There was hesitancy in her eyes. Perhaps Matthew was misreading her tired expression.

Or maybe he'd been right earlier, and something odd had happened when she went to Mami's shop alone.

# 26

*Madeline. Madeline. Madeline.*

Charli's best friend's name echoed in her mind, Mami's voice mocking her. She'd been trying to avoid the memory, but now that she had to meet Mami Watu again, there was no escaping.

And this time, Charli would not be meeting Mami in search of helpful information. She had to interrogate her. That would require focus on Charli's part, and she was already sleep-deprived. If Charli didn't shake off her doubts, she'd be off her game, which meant she couldn't avoid facing her thoughts any longer. The situation had to be analyzed.

Charli let Matthew drive, something she rarely did. Matthew was a bit of a speed demon, and Charli preferred to obey all traffic laws religiously. But Matthew driving would give her time to think.

"Is everything okay with you?" Matthew glanced at Charli before redirecting his eyes back to the road.

Charli shrugged. "Just tired."

*Ahem.*

Charli let out a long, slow breath. Her partner could tell

when she was lying. He always did. And the way he had cleared his throat indicated his doubt. But she didn't want to discuss this with him. Not until she figured out on her own what it all meant.

There were only two ways that Mami Watu could have known Madeline's name, the first one being that Mami Watu knew more about Charli than she let on. She couldn't have found this information about Charli online, but perhaps she knew someone who had gone to high school with her. It wouldn't be impossible to find Madeline and Charli's link, even if it was difficult.

The other option, the one Charli did not want to believe, was that voodoo was real. That Mami Watu really had convened with the spirit world to discover this truth about Charli.

A chill ran down her spine. Not because magic freaked her out or anything. No, that wasn't the problem.

*What if there really was a spirit world? Was Madeline's soul out there somewhere? Could she be watching Charli right now? And if so, what did she think of her life? Did she remember that Charli had failed to help her?*

A million questions swirled through Charli's mind, and none of them put her at ease. The second Mami had spoken Madeline's name, Charli began to entertain this disturbing possibility.

Truth be told, Charli was relieved Cedric had said Tany Speers was Mami's mentor. It was the first moment Charli considered that Mami Watu was not as honest and kind as she claimed. And if she wasn't, if she was underhanded, she could have been working hard to discover details about Charli's life. Charli could rule out all this spiritual nonsense in that case.

Her reasoning would open a new can of worms. If Mami was lying and had gone to the trouble of digging dirt on

Charli, then she obviously had something to hide. Could it be that Mami herself was directly involved with these deaths? She certainly had a love for voodoo dolls, even if they were more exquisite than the ones found on the victims.

"Look, I know something is wrong. Just tell me what it is." Matthew's words jolted Charli out of her head and back into the real world.

She let out a long shaky breath. "It's a lot to explain."

"Try me."

Perhaps it would be beneficial to talk to Matthew about what had happened. What could it hurt to get it off her chest?

"You know how Mami Watu wanted to give me a free reading?"

"Yeah." Matthew turned onto the road that would eventually lead to Mami Watu's shop.

"Well, I figured I'd let her do one. She'd been helpful with the case, and I didn't want any bad blood. And she told me a lot of things would be easily guessed. That I'm a workaholic and don't take enough time for myself."

"Doesn't take a psychic to tell you that."

"No. But then, completely out of nowhere, she told me that a woman named Madeline was on my mind."

Matthew's mouth fell open. "What?"

"Yeah. That was my reaction too. It really freaked me out."

"You don't think it means anything, though. Right? She had to have known about Madeline."

Charli squeezed her eyes shut. That was exactly what she wanted to believe. But what if there was some truth to voodoo magic? Her silence spoke volumes.

"Charli, of course it doesn't mean anything. Why have you been so rattled lately? This case is really getting to you."

He wasn't wrong. "I don't know why. It's not the most disturbing case I've ever seen. I mean, I didn't relish seeing

Dawn pinned up in her living room like that. But I've been bothered since before we visited that crime scene."

"You're tired. You need to get more sleep. And it wouldn't hurt to take time for yourself."

Charli rolled her eyes at her partner even though she knew he was focused on the road. "You're one to talk."

Matthew was just as much a workaholic as Charli was. Hell, he may be worse than Charli because he'd been doing detective work for a good ten years longer than she had.

"True, and my failed trip to California to see Chelsea doesn't make me want to jump on a plane again. We've had big case after big case. The stress is getting to us both."

Charli smacked the dash. "No, it isn't. I'm doing just fine. I can do my job even when I've had a big caseload."

She scorned any implication that she couldn't handle her workload. Even if Matthew was only trying to help, Charli filtered his words to mean she wasn't doing a good enough job.

Matthew's mouth set in a thin line. His shoulders tensed, and his hands gripped the wheel a little tighter.

She should probably apologize for the attitude, but apologies weren't easy for Charli to offer. Instead, she softened her voice and changed the subject.

"Do you think there is a possibility that Mami Watu is working with Tany Speers?"

"Who's to say? I mean, we've got no information on this Speers woman. Technically, she isn't even real. At least, she doesn't have that name. I'm still leaning toward Carl being responsible. It makes sense that he'd go for Dawn after he heard she confessed about his voodoo doll purchase."

But Charli wasn't buying it. Things weren't clicking with Carl being the one responsible. She wasn't writing off the possibility, of course. And if he had left tonight to kill Dawn

Rita, he'd likely be caught when he tried to return to his apartment.

He didn't seem capable of such a brutal murder, though. Even if he had the will to kill Jefferson for what happened to his son, it seemed like a stretch that he would brutally murder Dawn and pin her up to the wall.

Mami Watu, on the other hand, had actively tried to manipulate Charli. She went out of her way to disturb her with the free reading and Madeline's name. And that was in addition to the deception around Tany.

"What did Mami have to say about Madeline?" Matthew itched to get answers.

"How do you mean? She just mentioned her name."

"But in what context? It wasn't like she dropped it out of nowhere."

A long groan escaped Charli. "She said that Madeline was the reason I'm never able to slow down from my job."

"Hmm."

"Hmm?" Charli turned to Matthew, arms folded.

"It's just that there probably is truth to that."

Charli knew it, but she didn't need Matthew's words making it more real for her. Because, in the back of her mind, that was why she couldn't deny the possibility of voodoo being real.

Even if Mami Watu did her due diligence and found out about Madeline, how did she know Madeline was the reason Charli could never take a break? She could have guessed that, but it was as if Mami had infiltrated Charli's mind. Somehow, she knew that if Charli ever took time to herself, the empty hours brought her back to memories of Madeline.

Matthew patted Charli's shoulder, keeping one hand on the steering wheel, and it took all her willpower not to pull away. "I'm just saying, Charli, it doesn't hurt to take a vacation now and again. The world won't stop if you leave. You might be our best detective, but you're not our only detective. We would make it without you."

But it wasn't about that for Charli. She was aware the precinct would do just fine without her. The issue was Charli wouldn't be fine without the precinct.

Matthew tapped the steering wheel, his mouth opening, but no words came out. *Whew.* Charli breathed a sigh of relief. They'd arrived at Mami Watu's shop. When Matthew moved to release his seat belt, Charli put her hand up.

"Wait, I think I should go in there alone."

"You do?"

"Before I can interrogate Mami, I need to get this Madeline business out of the way. And it'll be easiest to do that one-on-one."

Matthew leaned back in his seat. "Whatever you think, Charli. I'll be here waiting if you need me."

Charli flashed him a smile. "Thanks."

Despite the stressful situation, there was comfort in having such a considerate partner. Matthew was more than a partner, but a best friend. And she was lucky to have him.

But whatever comfort he was able to provide with his kindness dissipated as soon as Charli clicked the buzzer to ring up to Mami Watu's apartment. The moment her finger touched that button, a blanket of ice enveloped her body.

*This wasn't going to go well.*

# 27

In a red floral nightgown that flowed behind her in the night breeze, Mami Watu opened the front door. She rubbed her tired eyes as she took in Charli's presence.

"Detective, what are you doing here?"

"I need to speak to you urgently."

Mami leaned against the doorjamb, looking weary. "It can't wait until morning?"

Charli kept her arms by her side, one hand tucked into the front pocket of her pants. A stab of guilt hit her. Maybe she shouldn't have called on the woman this late at night. But she'd already woken her up, and Charli's gut screamed that her questions couldn't wait. "No, I'm sorry. Can we talk now?"

Mami straightened and slowly turned around, waving Charli in. "I'm afraid I'm not prepared to offer you any tea."

Charli shut the door behind her, locking the cool air away. "I don't need tea, just you. Would you like to speak up in your apartment or remain here?"

Mami shivered in her nightgown. "We can go sit in my

office. No need to drag you all the way upstairs to my mess of a home."

That was odd. There was no way Mami Watu's home was a mess. Not when her shop was so impeccably pristine. *Was there evidence in her apartment she didn't want Charli to see?*

Charli wouldn't push it. If she pried too much, Mami Watu would be resistant to the conversation, and she was already pushing her luck by visiting the woman so late.

Aside from wanting to learn what Mami had hidden in her home, Charli wished she'd been invited up to avoid the office. As soon as the lights flashed on, the memory of her reading collapsed onto her. The echo of Madeline's name knocked the wind from her lungs. Charli sucked in a ragged breath.

"Detective Cross, are you okay?" Mami tilted her head, her eyes boring into Charli's soul.

Was her concern genuine? Or was this all an act created to disarm Charli further?

Charli straightened her back. "How did you know about Madeline?"

Being blunt was the only way forward here. Charli needed to get the upper hand again. And the way to do that was to let her know she was suspicious of that reading from earlier. From the first time they had met, Mami Watu oozed confidence that her image as a successful businesswoman would shield her from skepticism. Not with Charli, though. Not anymore.

"You came here in the middle of the night to ask about your reading?" Mami Watu attempted to flip the script.

A light bulb came on in Charli's mind. *How could she not have seen what Mami was trying to do?* Charli couldn't believe it hadn't hit her earlier. Everything with Mami Watu was a power play. The gaunt woman was vying to be in control of this narrative.

"No, but I think it needs to be addressed. What do you know about Madeline?"

"Nothing." Mami pressed her palms together as if in prayer, her expression serene. "I didn't even have a last name. It was only the first name that came to me. And I never intended to bother you. My only goal with my readings is to bring my clients clarity."

Charli stared at the older woman, wishing she could climb inside her mind. She was certain Mami had an ulterior motive at play. Charli couldn't force the woman to admit to anything she didn't want to, though. But it didn't matter. She didn't have to. The important thing was Charli was now aware deceit was at play.

"Fine, never mind that. Let's talk about your relationship with Dawn."

"Dawn Rita? We barely have one. I told you already that she comes into my shop from time to time." Mami Watu straightened out her nightgown where it met the blue chair cushion.

Charli sank into her own seat. "You also made it clear that you don't like her. I'm wondering how deep your tension with Dawn runs."

"Well, certainly not that deep." Mami Watu waved a dismissive hand. "I don't appreciate the way she practices voodoo, but that's it. It's not as if there is a personal vendetta between us. I doubt she even knows I dislike her."

"Oh, but she does. Detective Church and I met with her yesterday, and she didn't seem to care for you, either."

Mami Watu's eyes narrowed. "I'm sorry, Detective, but I'm just not understanding how any of this applies to your case. Did you discover Dawn has something to do with your victim in the cemetery? Because if so, I assure you we've never worked together."

There was something about the way Mami Watu squinted

at her that rang disingenuously. "Are you sure you don't know how it's relevant?"

"Of course not. How would I know?"

With all the police surrounding Dawn's home, there were surely neighbors on Old Burn Road who were aware of Dawn's passing. Any one of them could have called Mami and informed her. Or, even worse, Mami could have been directly involved herself.

"I am afraid Dawn was found dead tonight." Charli purposefully left out the fact that the death had been a murder. She wanted to leave things open so that if Mami did know something, there was room for her to incriminate herself.

Mami shut her eyes and placed a gentle hand on her chest. "Another one gone to Papa Legba's will. I am sorry to hear that. I may not have much liked Dawn, but I would never wish death on her. What happened?"

"I'm not at liberty to disclose details. But I need to know where you were tonight between seven and nine-thirty p.m."

"I had a class tonight starting at six that ran late, to about eight thirty. It's a small course for women seeking a priestess to mentor them as they dive further into our religion. I'd be happy to get you in contact with any of them to confirm that. And afterward, I went up to my apartment to relax before bed."

"Was anyone with you?"

"No, Detective. I live alone. But a few of the young women watched me lock up and walk upstairs. I'm sure if you were to search my internet records, you could find that I was sending off a few emails from my home IP."

There was no sense of alarm in Watu's eyes. She was cool as a cucumber, a bastion of calm. Could Charli be off base? *Maybe Mami was simply a successful businesswoman and a pillar of the voodoo community in Savannah.*

It wasn't as though Charli had anything concrete on Mami Watu. If anything, the evidence still pointed to Carl Perkins. There was nothing but Charli's gut instinct, and normally, she'd never trust such a thing. It was Matthew who relied on his intuition to solve cases, not Charli. She followed the facts.

But she'd been so…off the past couple of days. Even the way she approached her case was shifting for reasons she couldn't explain. If Charli had to make a guess, though, it likely had something to do with the earlier reading she had experienced with the priestess.

Heaviness settled in her chest, threatening to overflow. Charli couldn't shake her frustration. Her heart ached for her best friend, and she loathed that Mami Watu had used her name in her reading. It was possible this mix of emotions was causing Charli to be more suspicious of Mami than she should be. Sorting through her feelings to figure out if her skepticism was unfounded was a difficult task.

But there was one lie Charli was positive the older woman had told.

"What about Tany?" The words tumbled from the detective's mouth.

"E-Excuse me?"

That was odd. It was almost imperceptible, but Charli could have sworn Mami had just slurred her speech.

"Tany Speers. Do you know how we can get in touch with her?"

"I already told you, I don't." Mami crossed her ankles and settled back in her chair.

"But I'm thinking that isn't true. You know Tany a little better than you let on. She was your mentor, wasn't she?"

Mami's lips parted, her hands fidgeting in her lap. Finally, something Charli said had unnerved her.

"Who told you that?"

"I don't think the question is *who* told me. I'd rather know *why* you kept that fact hidden."

Mami Watu drew in a deep breath. "I'll admit that, yes, Tany Speers trained me. I did omit that part. But you have to understand this was decades ago. At the time, I didn't know what I was getting myself into when I started working with Tany. It took me years to see how conniving and manipulative that woman was."

"Even so, why would you hide your relationship with her?"

"Because her reputation and mine are as different as could be. I didn't want people associating me or my shop with witches like Tany Speers. Her name invokes fear in this city, Detective. Nobody would come to my shop if they believed we had a connection."

That was probably true. Charli had learned a lot about Tany, and none of it was good. It made sense that Mami might need to put space between herself and the voodoo priestess.

"It's no justification for lying to a detective." Charli may have been softening toward the idea that Mami Watu was innocent, but she wasn't going to let her know that. She had to keep the pressure on, just in case.

"No, you are right." Mami lowered her head. "And I apologize for that. I have a lot of shame about my time with Tany, and I let it cloud my judgment. But I didn't lie about not knowing how to contact her anymore. Nobody who knows her location will share it with me. I actually tried to get in touch with her after you came to speak to me."

Charli folded her arms, flicking at a minuscule piece of lint on her jacket. "Why would you do that?"

Mami lifted her chin. "Because, Detective, I strongly suspect that she is involved with your case. And I am tired of the horrendous crimes she inflicts on the community of

Savannah. That woman deserves to be behind bars, and I'm happy to help with that in any way possible."

"In that case, could you tell me her real name?" Charli pulled out her notepad.

Mami tilted her head. "Excuse me? Are you suggesting that Tany Speers is not her real name?"

"There's definitely no Tany Speers on record here in Savannah."

Mami Watu's eyes darted around the room. "Then I simply don't know, Detective Cross. She never even implied to me that she had a different legal name. Tany Speers is all I know. I wish I could be of more help to you. Believe me, I do."

Charli didn't want to believe her. If Mami had no part in this crime and actually wanted to help, it meant she didn't have another motive for dropping Madeline's name. And if she wasn't trying to use Madeline to rattle Charli, did it mean that the name really came to her unprompted?

A pit formed in Charli's stomach. She couldn't keep coming back to these thoughts. Madeline was gone, and she wasn't speaking to Charli from the underworld via Mami Watu. She couldn't be. The idea was insane.

Still, Charli couldn't let her fears impact her case. She had no evidence against Mami. There was no sense in beating this dead horse. And it was better to keep the woman on her side, considering her deep connections with Savannah's voodoo community.

"Will you continue to try reaching out to Tany Speers?" Charli's voice softened.

"Of course. I haven't stopped trying to get ahold of her. But I wouldn't hold your breath, Detective. I know Tany, so I know how good she is at covering her tracks. If she doesn't want to be found, I won't be able to find her."

Serenity settled on Mami's face. It was best for Charli to

end this interrogation now, while she was still on the woman's good side. Guilty or not, she wanted Mami open to working with her.

"I appreciate your help, regardless. My apologies for waking you up so late." Charli rose from her chair. "I'll be in touch."

"Absolutely. It was not a problem." Mami accompanied Charli to the door.

The priestess followed Charli to the entrance, and she rested a hand on the detective's arm. A shudder ran through Charli.

"Detective, I just want to tell you again how sorry I am for startling you earlier. You aren't the first person I've terrified, and you won't be the last. But my goal is never to enact scare tactics with my clients. I do hope you'll remain open to readings in the future."

That was highly unlikely. Charli hadn't wanted to do the reading in the first place, but after that experience, she wanted nothing to do with fortune-telling.

*Was Mami Watu being genuinely nice, or was she searching for another opportunity to rattle and distract her?*

Only time would tell.

# 28

My fingers slipped through the silky hair of the new doll. They were going to love this one. Her pale blue eyes almost glowed in the lamplight. She was one of my most glorious creations. I caressed the doll's short black hair, causing it to lay in the same way *she* wore it.

I set her down on the cluttered coffee table next to a wheel of hemp rope and my lighter. The whistle of the teakettle filled my small home. I rose to my feet to take it off the gas stove.

After all that had happened tonight, I was desperate for a cup of tea. Deep in my soul, I was sure I'd done right by ridding this community of Dawn Rita. The witch had gotten what she deserved, and I would never apologize for playing a part in her death.

What had me shaken, though, was the way in which she died. I wasn't sure what I expected from the monster, but it wasn't that. He'd implemented a brutality I'd never before witnessed.

A shiver whispered through me.

My soul never relished the murders I had to commit.

They were a necessity, a means to an end. I was confident I was doing the will of Papa Legba. There were sacrifices that had to be made in the name of community. I didn't needlessly torture, though.

But I feared that was exactly what had happened to Dawn. I'd invited the monster into her home, and he did what monsters do. I preferred a painless, clean death, similar to the one I'd given Jefferson. When he left this earthly realm, it was as though he could have been sleeping. My firm belief was that we all deserved a painless death no matter how great our past crimes may have been.

But the monster had no soul. And I had no control over him.

*Was it a mistake to invite him with me? Even worse, had I made a grave error in judgment when I asked for his protection?*

A series of clean but cluttered teacups decorated my countertops. I grabbed a handful of loose-leaf tea and scooped it into my shaker before adding the boiling water. With trembling fingers, I reached for the kettle, my hand almost too weak to bear its weight.

Using both hands, I poured the steaming water into a cup, water sloshing violently over the top. Eucalyptus rushed against my face and cooled my shamed skin. If only it could calm my shamed soul as well.

I wouldn't let it happen again. Perhaps I would be required to kill another. That couldn't be helped. But I could ensure that death was never so brutal again.

The images of Dawn's mangled body haunted my mind. I feared if I didn't cast a spell to remove it, she'd be in my nightmares for months to come. Her severed limbs would return to life and dance toward me with reckless abandon.

It was one thing to chop her up after her passing. That was what I assumed would happen to her after her poisoning. But she had been frozen in time as the beast ripped her apart. Her spirit endured the horror while her physical body was helpless to prevent the agony she endured.

Regret filled my soul, and I cursed my curiosity. *What had possessed me to peek through that window?*

Nausea bubbled up at the mere thought of the scene, and I sipped my tea, willing the eucalyptus to calm my aching stomach. Though even if it did, that would only be a bandage. The pain would resurface for as long as my guilt remained.

And it wouldn't be enough to wipe my mind of it. No, I had to provide more. When someone passed within the grip of horrendous turmoil, it could affect their entry into the underworld. And to experience the underworld in chaos would prevent internal peace from being achieved in the afterlife.

I took my tea to the coffee table and moved the replica of the witch onto my couch. The spell required space. Black-and-white candles lined my coffee table, and I placed them into a star formation before lighting each one.

A piece of Dawn's hair remained in my possession, and I set it in the middle of the shape. Faint candlelight reflected against my dim walls. The flickering light was small at first but grew as Papa Legba's presence rose within me.

"Papa Legba, I ask for your forgiveness. Please allow Dawn Rita to pass into your domain with peace in her soul. Guide her into your world, for she has done wrong but should be allowed to make her sins right. Settle the spirit who once owned the hair I hold before me."

A gust of air blew out each candle in one fell swoop, and relief swept through me just as quickly. Papa Legba had agreed to my requests. If nothing else, I could rest at ease that Dawn's suffering had passed.

With the passing of her torture, I could redirect my attention to the pain of others. There were more people who needed to be calmed. More wretched individuals who deserved a course correction. Before it was too late.

My attention traveled back to the pixie-haired doll. *She* had to be my next correction. I sat back on my couch, my hands curving around the doll that so closely resembled her. I made sure the face had the same cold, dark expression I'd seen her wear during press briefings.

All my focus had to be on redirecting her. I'd thrown every spell within my book of knowledge her way, but to no avail. Her aura was gaining on me.

I had only one more chance to prevent her from discovering me without resorting to violence.

If this spell didn't work, I'd have no choice. I'd have to take drastic measures.

# 29

Charli covered her mouth with a hand, a yawn escaping her lips.

"You sure you're good to drive?" Matthew handed Charli the keys as she left Mami Watu's shop.

"I'm fine. I'm dropping you off then going straight home to sleep. Any news about Carl?"

Matthew shut the passenger door. "The officer in front of his house hasn't seen him coming or leaving."

"Then we will have to wait until tomorrow. We've got no evidence to go knocking his door down, and we both need the sleep."

Matthew yawned, resting his head on the seat. "You can say that again. I'm pretty sure I dozed off while you were in there with Mami Watu. Find anything interesting?"

"Not really. She admitted that she lied about Tany Speers but said she wanted to keep a degree of separation from her because of her business reputation. Despite my accusations, she was completely calm."

Matthew shrugged. "I'm telling you, it's gotta be Carl running this show. He's the only one with a clear-cut motive.

I mean, sure, we know Dawn and Mami didn't like each other, but that's hardly a reason for murder."

Matthew wasn't wrong, but Charli still wasn't going to close off any possibilities. Mami Watu, Carl Perkins, and this mysterious Tany Speers were still all on the table in her mind.

"She swears she doesn't know Tany's real name or location, unfortunately. I'm starting to think we're never going to find this woman. It's like she never even existed." Charli reached for the radio. Maybe the music would wake her up.

"Maybe she never did." Matthew spread out his fingers and waved them around, as if he was telling a mysterious ghost story.

It wasn't the first time the thought had crossed Charli's mind, though. Never had someone lived in Savannah and remained so well hidden. *Was it really possible that not a single soul was aware of how to get in touch with Tany?*

Charli considered bringing this up to Matthew as a serious possibility, but she was too tired for a long conversation. She needed to get home, and she still had to get Matthew back to his apartment first. Thankfully, he only lived about ten minutes from the Historic District where Charli resided.

They rode the rest of the way in comfortable silence, only breaking it to say their goodbyes in Matthew's parking lot. As soon as he exited, Charli blasted the radio to an obscene volume. The steering wheel rattled under her palms. She'd never turned the speakers up this loud, but the weight of her exhaustion was getting to her. Anything that would jolt her awake was a good idea.

Charli steered her car into her driveway, reaching to turn off the ignition. She froze.

*What the hell?*

A shadowy figure was planted on her porch. All remnants

of sleepiness evaporated in an instant, her heart threatening to beat out of her chest.

She didn't get many visitors at home, even in the middle of the day. *Why on earth would someone be standing on her porch in the wee hours of the morning?*

Charli sucked in a deep breath. She eased open her door, her hand on her gun as she approached the figure.

Once her feet hit the pathway to her entrance, the motion sensors on her porch lit up and exposed the man in front of her.

Preston Powell leaned against her door, a sly grin on his face.

"And here I thought you were inside ignoring me."

Charli released the breath she'd held since she left her car. "How long have you been here?"

"Just a few minutes. I had a late night and figured with your case, maybe you had too. Thought perhaps we could both take the edge off with a drink."

The only thing Charli wanted to take the edge off with was a nap. She wouldn't go to sleep after Preston had startled her like that, though.

"I'm not much of a drinker, actually. I don't ever go to the bar to blow off steam."

This wasn't a blow off. Charli hadn't yet decided whether she was going to reject Powell. She was simply too tired not to be honest.

"It doesn't have to be at a bar." Preston stepped closer, and the porch light gleamed off his perfect white teeth.

Charli eyed the handsome agent up and down. "Preston, what are you really doing here?"

"I'm taking a chance. I figured if either one of us was going to, it had to be me."

It could've been the lack of sleep making her sensitive, but Charli resented the implication that she wasn't a risk-taker. Was Powell off in his perceptions of her, though? When was the last time she'd done something adventurous? And he likely wasn't wrong that if he didn't pursue her, she never would've called him herself.

"But what are you hoping will happen here tonight?"

Preston shrugged. "I've got no expectations, Charli. I only want to spend time with the gorgeous, intelligent woman I had the pleasure of working with a few weeks ago."

This couldn't have come at a worse time. Charli suppressed a groan, wishing she had time to mull over the decision of whether or not to move forward with Preston, and she had no time to do so now. Not to mention she could barely keep her eyes open. It was tempting to wave off Preston with the excuse of needing rest, though she'd likely be up for the next hour after her adrenaline spike.

If she blew him off now, it would probably be the last time he sought her out. A man could only be rejected so many times before he gave up. Charli may not have decided whether she wanted Preston, but she wasn't ready to let him walk away for good.

"You know, I've been up for the past few days with only short blocks of sleep." Whatever Charli decided, Preston should be aware of this. She wouldn't be very exciting company tonight.

"I get it. You need to get your rest. It's not a problem."

And there it was. The decision had been made for her. Preston had made an assumption, and he was already making his way down her porch. Charli could step into her house and not have to worry about this any longer.

Charli faced her front door for a moment before turning on her heel. "Wait, Preston?"

When he turned around, hopeful eyes beckoned her forward. "Yes?"

"I can't stay up too late, and I've only got half a bottle of wine in the fridge. But you're welcome to come in for a bit."

The dimples in his cheeks popped with his grin. "I'd love to."

*See, she could still be spontaneous.*

There was an adventurous spirit in her heart after all these years. That same heart was about to pound out of her chest with anxiety, but maybe the wine would help with that.

Preston followed her to the kitchen, and she pulled two wine glasses from the cabinet, setting them on her round kitchen table. It was small, but big enough for two people to sit down for a meal.

"You look stunning tonight, by the way." Preston reached for his glass after Charli poured a quarter of the rose-colored bottle into it.

Charli snorted with laughter. "You're kidding, right? I don't think I've showered since yesterday."

Not exactly the most romantic thing to say on a date. *Was this a date?* Even if it wasn't, Charli should choose her words more carefully. There was no sense in self-sabotage.

"You manage to make a hard day's work look beautiful, I suppose."

There it was again. Preston seemed to know the way to Charli's heart. It wasn't just in complimenting her looks, but a quality more tangible. Her intelligence, her work ethic, her skills as a detective, those were the only kind of compliments that could make her swoon.

Preston interrupted her thoughts as he leaned against the kitchen island. "How is your case going, by the way?"

Relief flowed through Charli. This was something she could answer. "It's been frustrating, actually. Digging into all this voodoo magic is spinning my head in a way my cases usually don't."

"I'm sure you'll find your footing soon enough. You are

undeniably talented." Preston moved in closer to Charli. His spicy cologne penetrated her air space in an unexpectedly sexy way.

Her breath hitched. His proximity was a magnet, drawing her closer to him. It had been so long since she'd been with a man.

Doubts began to creep into her mind. What if they ended up in her bedroom? She was more than a little out of practice, and she hadn't showered or shaved her legs or...

*Stop it.*

Normally, Charli didn't find physical intimacy particularly daunting. If it had been another man standing so close in her kitchen, she would be unfazed.

But she'd worked with Preston. They were talking about her job, something Charli never did with hookups because her career was too complicated to explain. He knew her analytical mind, and he appreciated her for it.

The emotional closeness was what had her scared. Her eyes drifted toward her back door, tempted to sprint to it and make her escape.

Until she reminded herself that Preston was only here for a short time. Their relationship would never be serious. The distance would always be a barrier. This fact was what Charli needed to remember to move forward. She didn't want to dive into a relationship with Preston, but she could do a fling.

"How did you find my address, anyway?" The question wasn't an accusation but a flirtation.

Preston winked, leaning in closer. "Turns out you're not the only genius detective in Savannah."

Charli chuckled. "Are you sure that's not an abuse of your power?"

"No. And I'm not sure this isn't, either."

He reached for her chin, tilting her face toward his.

Callused fingertips caressed her cheek as his mouth lowered, his warm breath grazing her skin. All at once, his lips were on hers.

*Mmmm.* She kissed him back, hard. Charli's stomach fluttered as she pulled her mouth from his with a soft smile.

Whether it was the wine or her tired haze lending her courage, she didn't care.

"Would you like to come with me upstairs?"

# 30

*Beep. Beep. Beep. Beep.*

Charli's alarm sounded just a few hours after she fell asleep. She rolled over, pressing the snooze button with a groan. She'd slept like a rock, but with the sleep debt she'd gotten herself into, the few hours weren't nearly enough.

Snoring next to her, Preston didn't awake to the sound of the alarm. If she didn't know better, Charli would assume he was comatose.

Now that the wine had worn off and she'd gotten a few hours of sleep, she doubted her choices from the night before. Why had she been so quick to invite Preston into her bed? They'd barely spoken for ten minutes before they were fumbling up the stairs to her room, locked together by their lips.

If the night had been satisfying, Charli might not be doubting her decisions. But it had been nothing to write home about. That might not be entirely Preston's fault, though. Once they got going, Charli was so tired that every movement of her body became a monumental effort. It wasn't easy to relax into the moment when every muscle in your body ached.

At least the exercise had knocked her out cold. A dreamless sleep befell her, and she needed that even more than sex. Thank you for that, Preston Powell.

Now, it was time for him to leave.

Why did the morning after have to be so awkward? Charli had hoped he wouldn't stay the night, but she'd drifted off so fast she didn't have time to suggest he leave. At least he'd understand that she needed to get to work early. He probably needed to take off soon for his own case as well.

But to send the agent on his merry way, Charli had to wake him, something she didn't relish. All it would take was a simple nudge on the shoulder, but once he woke, she'd have to have a conversation about the previous night.

What would she even say? Was last night as drab for him as it was for her? That would be the best-case scenario, so there would be no expectation of hooking up again.

The heavy yellow-and-green striped duvet was suffocatingly hot as the morning sun rose outside her window. *Crap.* The sun meant it was at least seven, and Charli had planned to be at the precinct by now. Luckily, she didn't have a briefing she had to get to, so it didn't matter if she was later than normal, especially after her late-night visit with Mami.

Charli pushed the comforter halfway off her body, forcing it slightly off Preston as well. Either her movement or the cool air on his bare back caused him to stir. For the first time, Charli considered that the rest of him might be unclothed too. Heat crept into Charli's cheeks.

*Fantastic.*

Powell rolled over, a sleepy grin on his lips. "Hey, gorgeous."

"Good morning." She ran a hand through her hair, trying

to tame what probably looked like a porcupine intent on throwing its quills. "Hope you slept well."

What a dumb thing to say to someone she'd just had sex with.

"I definitely did. Last night was fantastic."

Dammit, their experiences didn't align. But what could Charli say? It would only make things even more uncomfortable if she admitted that last night wasn't worth the lost sleep.

"Yeah, I'm glad you came over." The statement wasn't a complete lie. She did sleep really well after their, um, encounter.

"Me too. You've got a beautiful house, by the way."

"Thank you. It belonged to my grandmother. She left it to me."

Should she say something more? Ask him about his home? She groaned. Making small talk was the last thing on Charli's agenda right now.

"I knew it was a bit much on a detective's salary." It was a flirtatious tease, but Charli didn't want to flirt anymore.

Last night, she'd been able to move forward thanks to a glass of wine and the haze of her exhaustion. Now that she was sober and awake, this conversation couldn't be over soon enough.

For once, the universe threw her a bone. Her phone rang, and she was saved by the bell.

She practically lunged for the device. "Sorry, I have to take this."

Powell nodded before letting his head fall back on the pillow.

*Why was he still in the bed? Ugh, couldn't he just get up and leave already?*

Charli clicked to answer the call. "Detective Cross."

"I knew as soon as this gruesome body came through my doors that it must be a case of yours."

How was Soames calling her this early in the morning? The body would've come in during the middle of the night. "You've already had a chance to look at it?"

"I was working late on a smoke inhalation case but had to put that on pause once I saw it. I couldn't help myself."

Soames was just as much a workaholic as Charli. "Find anything interesting?"

"A couple things of interest, yes. The first being that, by the amount of blood present at the scene, the desecration of the body happened while she was still alive."

Charli's stomach flipped. That wasn't easy to process. Charli couldn't fathom the horror that Dawn had endured in her last moments.

"I assumed it had been after her death because the cuts were so clean. Wouldn't she have fought back?" It couldn't have been easy to chop up a woman who was struggling to get away.

"That brings me to my next point of interest. It appears your victim also consumed a significant amount of curare. Enough to paralyze her for the time it took to kill her."

That made the death even more heinous. The poor woman had to lie there frozen as immeasurable pain was inflicted upon her until she bled out?

Whoever had done this was severely twisted. Her manner of death was such a far cry from the way Jefferson died. He didn't have a single wound on his body.

"Detective, are you still there?"

*Silence.*

"Detective Cross?"

Charli jolted back to reality, forcing her mind back on track. "Why did you test for curare?"

"I had to do a tox screen on the blood sample, anyway. Since your last case involved curare, I thought it would be a good thing to add. Always the possibility the two cases could be related."

This was why Charli loved working with Soames. Like her, he always examined every angle. He was extremely effective in his work.

"You were definitely on the right track."

"I'd love to go over this with you and compare notes on Jefferson Brown's examination."

"That would be fantastic. I'll pick up Matthew, and we'll be there within the hour."

"See you then."

She tossed her phone on the chair and headed to the dresser for fresh underwear.

"So, I take it you're on your way out?"

Charli stopped mid step.

*Preston. Oh, crap.*

Charli had been so engrossed in her conversation with Soames she'd forgotten Preston was still there. Again.

*Please don't be awkward.*

"Yeah." She forced a bright smile onto her face. "We've got a big break in our case."

"Not a problem." His lips shifted into the same sexy smile he'd used on her earlier. "I should get to work myself. But I hope you and I will get to talk again soon."

*I hope we don't.*

Her jaw muscles began to stiffen, but she kept them in place. "I'm sure we will."

Preston leaned over to give Charli a kiss on the cheek before exiting the bed. He was wearing boxers. *Whew.* It didn't take long for him to throw on the rest of his clothes and head downstairs.

Charli sat there, his footsteps causing each stair to creak

on his way down. The door squeaked open before clicking closed. She breathed a sigh of relief.

Now that her interaction with Preston was officially over, she could focus on what mattered. She dialed Matthew.

*He'd better be awake.*

"What's up, Charli?"

"We've got to go meet with Soames. He's already finished his report on Dawn Rita."

"That was quick. And what did he find?"

"There was curare in her system. She was poisoned before her death and then painstakingly torn apart while she was still alive."

A small gagging noise came from the other end of the line. "That is…disgusting."

"It is. He wants to compare notes between Dawn Rita and Jefferson Brown. Can you be ready in thirty minutes?"

"Sure thing."

# 31

Charli and Matthew walked from her car to Dr. Soames's office in silence, each still processing what the M.E. had mentioned on the phone. Her partner shot her a strange look for the umpteenth time that morning.

His close inspection grated on her nerves. Charli whipped her head around. "What?"

"I don't know. You're just being really weird this morning."

*Weirder than normal?*

"No." The word shot out of her mouth like a rocket, and she forced a softer tone to finish the thought. "I'm not."

"Yes, you definitely are. Is this about your visit with Mami Watu?"

Actually, her jumpiness was about her visit with a certain GBI agent, but Charli didn't find it necessary to explain that little detail. She only needed a little time to shake off the events of the night.

Charli lifted her chin. "It's not. I'm over the reading."

Matthew didn't appear to be appeased by this, but he

opened the door to the medical examiner's office. Soames was already waiting to take them back to the body.

"Good to see you both. Wish it was under better circumstances. But then again, without a bad circumstance, I'd never get to see you at all."

Charli chuckled, a hint of a smile playing at her lips. Soames's sense of humor always managed to lift her spirits. For someone with such a dark job, he was constantly joking.

Parts of Dawn's body were arranged on a medical examination table. It was difficult to view the pieces of her, knowing that she was awake when this occurred. And if Charli was bothered, Matthew had to be even more perturbed. She glanced up at her partner.

Matthew averted his eyes, his face a chalky white. "I can't believe she was awake the whole time."

"Whoever got ahold of her definitely enjoyed taking the time to torture her slowly." Soames shuffled at the desk behind him to collect his notes.

"In that way, Moullette's death doesn't seem similar to Jefferson Brown at all, does it?" Charli walked around Dawn's reassembled body, deep sorrow for the pain the woman endured pounding in her chest.

Soames handed her two separate toxicology reports, one for Jefferson Brown and one for Dawn Rita. "No, it isn't. But the toxicology report sure is. Not only did they both consume curare, but we found trace amounts of barbiturates and psilocybin in both of them."

"Psilocybin, as in magic mushrooms?" Matthew shuddered. "You're telling me she was on hallucinogens at the time of her death too?"

Charli wrapped her arms around her body. *Could this case get any worse?* Being immobilized and hallucinating while having your body slashed apart had to be one of the most gruesome ways to die.

Soames could read the disgust on their faces. "If it's any comfort, I've seen research that psilocybin mushrooms can be very beneficial for accepting imminent death in terminal patients. It may have soothed her."

But terminal patients weren't being chopped into pieces while they tripped on magic mushrooms.

"At any rate, they were found in trace amounts."

A recent conversation with Mami Watu hit Charli like a ton of bricks. Hadn't she told Charli and Matthew she'd sold mushroom stems?

"Can we identify what mushroom did this?" Charli handed Matthew the toxicology reports.

"I'm afraid that psilocybin is in a wide variety of mushrooms. Since this was a small amount, it could be a genus that contains a low amount of psilocybin. But it could also mean she took a small amount of a more potent mushroom. Regardless, testing for psilocybin cannot lead us to a specific mushroom."

So, this couldn't provide concrete evidence of Mami Watu or anyone else's involvement, even if they found magic mushrooms on her person. But the link still stuck out to Charli. It was something they needed to investigate further.

"What is the exact cause of death?"

"Exsanguination."

Blood loss, exactly what she had expected. With how mauled her body was, Charli could only hope the poor lady had bled out quickly.

"Thank you for being so thorough. This is supremely helpful." Matthew handed the reports back to Soames.

"Of course. Call me any time with questions."

When they'd made it back outside, Matthew made a call to the officer who had been assigned to stake out Carl's home.

"Have you seen him?" Matthew paced back and forth with his cell on speakerphone.

"Actually, I just did. He left to grab himself a bagel from across the street. I stopped him and asked him about last night, but he said he was home. That checks out, considering I've been here all night and never saw him return."

Matthew sighed. "Okay, thanks. We'll be in touch with him."

Charli raised her hand to block the sun out of her eyes as she glanced up at Matthew. "Seems highly unlikely that Carl would have time to get back to the apartment after the murder without our officer noticing. The body was still warm when forensics was working on it."

Charli wasn't going to label the timeline as impossible. They'd have to dig deeper into the time it would take Carl to get home. But once they did, they could probably rule out Carl as a suspect. He lived in a third-floor apartment. It wasn't as if he could sneak by cops to get in through a back door. But a window?

"So that leaves us back at square one." Matthew shook his head in exasperation.

Charli understood his frustration, but it wasn't square one. All the information they had would serve as a road map. They only had to gather more facts to fill in the blanks.

"Let's talk with Dawn's neighbors on Old Burn Road. Maybe someone saw something or knows of Dawn Rita's enemies."

"It's a place to start."

If they were lucky, they just might get one step closer to solving this case.

# 32

Old Burn Road wasn't usually creepy in the daylight, but the night's horrific events lent an eerie aura.

Charli and Matthew had already knocked on a couple of doors to no answer. The citizens of Old Burn Road weren't exactly amenable to visits from cops. Although nothing about their clothes suggested they were officers of the law, word had already spread about Dawn Rita, and people appeared to be taking precautions when answering their doors.

Charli rubbed the back of her neck. *Was anyone going to talk to them?*

"Let's try this house next."

Matthew followed his partner's gaze. "If you can call that shack a house. I feel sorry for some of these people."

"I know. It makes me appreciate what I've got."

"And who you've got." Matthew fluttered his eyelashes, and Charli resisted the urge to poke him in the ribs. Her partner could always make her smile.

Charli knocked and waited a full thirty seconds before knocking again. "Please, someone answer."

An elderly woman with graying, unruly hair came to the door. She wore a dated burnt-orange blouse and a brown skirt that fell to her knees. "Hello?"

Charli made the introductions. "We were hoping you'd be able to help us with a case we're working on."

The woman stepped forward and shut the door behind her. "You're here about Dawn, aren't you?"

"We are, yes." Matthew stepped back, giving her room to move onto her porch.

"It's a tragedy. That's what that is. I heard you found her cut into pieces. Is that true?"

"I'm afraid we cannot discuss that." But Charli's answer was confirmation enough.

The woman shook her head. "I'm Louise Kane. Dawn and I were friends. Happy to tell you all I know, but I don't know much. I didn't hear a peep from her last night, and I had my living room windows open until ten when the police arrived. You'd think I would've heard a scream."

The curare must have been responsible for her silence. Dawn must've had paralysis in her facial muscles as well, unable to open her mouth to cry out.

"Even if you didn't hear anything last night, it would be great if you could tell us about Dawn. How was she viewed in the community? Did she have any enemies?" Charli had her notepad ready, her hand poised to scrawl.

Louise pushed her round wire-rimmed glasses up over the bridge of her nose. "I can't think of anyone who would've hurt Dawn. People loved her out here. Whenever anyone had a problem, they ran to Dawn. She'd help you solve it. Dawn helped me greatly when my son passed on. We sent a message to the great beyond to make sure he knew I still loved him."

"You're a believer in voodoo?" Every time Charli met

another follower, she held out hope they could lead her to Tany Speers.

"No, I'm a Christian woman, but Dawn never discriminated. She tried her best to support you no matter what you believed. That's what made her so special."

Mami Watu's description of Dawn was one of a woman who took advantage of the poor and suffering for financial gain. That was a far cry from the picture Louise had painted. But perhaps she was in the minority of people who liked Dawn. It was going to be difficult to figure that out if most of the neighbors wouldn't speak to them.

"And you believe that your other neighbors shared your positive feelings for Dawn?"

Louise used a loafer-clad toe to scratch her opposite ankle. "Absolutely! I've never heard anyone speak a bad word against that sweet woman."

Matthew huffed. "Funny, for people who liked her so much, nobody around here seems to want to help with our investigation."

Louise tucked her frizzy gray curls behind her ears. "You have to understand, Detectives, the police haven't been great to us out here. They come, and they take people away. But the police don't usually help us. It's not a reflection of how they feel about Dawn. And most of them, like me, probably don't think they can help much. None of them want to be wrapped up in this."

Charli leaned against the chipping white wood railing. "Do you know anything about Mami Watu or Tany Speers?"

Louise flung her hands on her hips, narrowing her eyes. "That Mami Watu is a whole heap of trouble. She doesn't do voodoo for the people like Dawn does. Mami has her shop, and she uses it to make money. Dawn is out in the trenches suffering alongside her community. Mami Watu walks around in her high heels, fancy suits, and she rubs her good fortune in everyone's face. At the end of the day, though, she's just jealous."

"Jealous of what?" Matthew glanced between Louise and Charli.

The woman huffed. "Jealous of Dawn, of course. Dawn had the love and attention of everyone."

Yet again, this didn't mesh with the image Mami Watu attempted to put on. Mami acted as though she was disgusted by Dawn, not envious of her. Dawn was supposed to be beneath her. Could it be that, in actuality, Dawn was more attuned with voodoo culture while Mami was focused on her profits?

"What about Tany Speers?" Matthew was the one to bring the name up, and Charli was grateful. She was so focused on Mami Watu, she'd nearly forgotten to ask.

Louise gave them a sideways glance. "Detective, come on. Surely you know about Tany."

Matthew met her gaze. "We've heard a lot of people speak about her, but I don't think I know what you're referencing."

Louise pushed her sliding glasses up on her face again. "Have you run into anyone who has actually met Tany?"

Was she implying that Tany wasn't real? The idea had crossed Charli's mind, but this was the first time someone had explicitly said it.

Charli ran down the list of people who had mentioned the elusive voodoo priestess. There was only one person who had claimed to have known Tany Speers. "Mami Watu asserted she was her mentor."

Louise scoffed, and for a moment, Charli thought the woman might spit on the porch. "Mami Watu is a deceitful woman. You cannot trust what she says."

Matthew put a hand up. "No, wait, Mami wasn't the only one. Dawn spoke of Tany too, didn't she?"

That was right. She'd been appalled when the detectives brought up Tany's name.

Louise bit her lower lip. "Dawn told me outright that Tany wasn't real. She knew who made up the myth of Tany. Never told me who, but she knew it was all fake."

Well, if that was true, that bit of information sure shifted things. If Tany wasn't real, why didn't Dawn admit that? She could've saved the detectives a whole lot of trouble.

"You know who else would talk to you? Mr. Siegel, two houses down. He's an honest man, no reason to fear cops. And he was healed by Dawn Rita. I know he'd love to help."

"Healed in what way?" Charli had learned a lot about voodoo in the past few days but had heard little about it healing ailments.

"She had a potion that took away his pain, and he's been very grateful to her ever since. He's retired, so he should be home right now."

The pieces of the puzzle were falling into place for Charli. In one crystallizing moment, everything began to make sense.

Charli handed Louise her card. "Which house did you say he was in?" She had no reason to continue this conversation. Her talk with Mr. Siegel was far more urgent.

"Two houses to the left." Louise tucked the business card in her pocket. "It's the lime green home. You can't miss it."

"Thank you, Louise. We appreciate you taking the time to talk to us." Charli resisted the urge to run down the steps instead of taking two at a time.

Matthew matched his partner's brisk strides. "You don't think we should ask her a few more questions? She seems to know Dawn pretty well." His footsteps were heavy against the cracked sidewalk.

"No need. We only need to confirm her story with Mr. Siegel."

Charli was glad she and Matthew were on the same wavelength. He might not know exactly what she had in mind, but he would allow her to process her thoughts without peppering her with questions.

Charli was already hopping onto Mr. Siegel's porch, pounding on the front door. Even if Matthew wanted to ask more questions, there wasn't another opportunity.

The door whipped open, and a man in his seventies stood before them. His head was balding, but the whiskers on his chin were snow white.

"Can I help you?"

"Hello, Mr. Siegel. We're investigating Dawn Rita's death. I'm Detective Cross, and this is my partner, Detective Church. We were told you might help with our investigation." Charli's words tumbled out, her chest heaving to catch her breath after her power walk.

"Please, call me Doug. But I doubt I can help you much. I wasn't home last night. Dreadful to hear what happened to Dawn, though. That woman has been great to me over the years."

"That's actually what we wanted to talk to you about. How do you know Dawn?" Charli almost didn't bother opening up her notebook, but she was too thorough of a detective not to jot down the conversation.

"We've been neighbors for nearly a decade, of course. But she helped me greatly with some pain I've been having. I've had arthritis for years." Doug held up his hands, displaying his swollen knuckles. "It pushed me into early retirement from my career as a plumber. My pain was so disabling that my doctors prescribed me a variety of drugs like Vicodin and codeine, but they never helped much at all. I'd spend my days in the bed, unable to do anything."

"That sounds awful." Though Matthew's words were

sympathetic, Charli suspected he was suspicious of why she was pressing so hard.

"It was. Dawn heard of my anguish, and she reached out to me. She gave me an herbal concoction that I can consume daily but won't cloud my head. It's changed my life."

That was exactly the confirmation Charli needed. "Do you happen to have any of these herbs on your person?"

"No, actually, I ran out yesterday." Doug's shoulders slumped, the despair rolling off him in waves. "Dawn was supposed to provide me with a new supply, but that won't be happening anymore."

Matthew gave a polite smile. "With Dawn Rita gone, maybe Mami Watu could provide you with these herbs."

Even before the older man's eyes widened incredulously, Charli was certain these were herbs Mami would never provide.

"That woman doesn't give you anything that actually helps. She has silly little tea packets that do nothing. Nobody out here on Old Burn believes in Mami Watu."

*Because Mami Watu would never sell the kinds of herbs Dawn was providing?*

"How would you describe your relationship with Dawn? Are you a customer?" Charli tapped her finger against her thigh. She was eager to move to her next interview, but she had to be thorough.

"No, I think we were friends."

"When was the last time you saw her?" The rickety porch boards creaked under Matthew's boot as he shifted in place.

"Last week, she dropped off the herbs for me. Our interactions were pretty short these days, actually. She'd come drop off herbs and then be on her way."

*Was it a friend dropping off herbs to a neighbor in need or a drug dealer visiting a client?*

Charli handed him a card. "Thank you for your time, Doug. If we have any other questions, we'll be reaching out." She was just as eager to leave as she had been at Louise's home.

"I'll be here." Doug moved back into the house, and Charli was already on her way to the car.

"Okay, wait a damn minute, Charli. I know that big brain of yours is hard at work, but slow down!"

"I can't!" Urgency made her feet go faster. She needed to act now before another person died. "We need to head back to town right now. I'll explain everything in the car."

"Okay, I trust you." He hopped into the passenger seat. "But just tell me one thing. Should I be worried about you? You've acted a little strange the past few days."

At another time, the question might offend Charli. But nothing could bother her right now. Her mind was too focused on the task at hand. Besides, Matthew wasn't wrong. She'd been a mess lately.

But that had nothing to do with this. Charli might appear manic, but this wasn't mania. It was the culmination of all their evidence falling into place.

"I'm perfectly fine, Matt."

Matthew flashed her a grin. "I can't wait to hear what you're thinking. Are you at least going to tell me where we're going?"

Yeah...she could do that much.

"We have to visit Mami Watu."

# 33

The aroma of sage and eucalyptus hit Charli as soon as she rushed through the door of Mami's shop. Matthew was close behind, standing near the door in case anyone wanted to pull any funny business.

Charli glanced around the empty shop. "Mami Watu? Are you here?" Anticipation coursed through Charli's veins. Still, she kept her voice calm and friendly.

Above her head, floorboards creaked just before Mami's high heels clacked on the stairwell.

"My apologies, Detectives." Mami wore a bright smile, but her face appeared haggard after their late-night visit. "The shop is usually empty around this time, so I went upstairs to fix myself an early lunch."

Her perfectly pleasant demeanor would not fool Charli, but she smiled back warmly. It was important to put any interviewee at ease, even the ones you suspected were cold-blooded murderers.

"That's not a problem. We're hoping you can help with a few things. Is it okay if my partner records this conversation?"

Mami inclined her head, almost like a queen to a servant. "Of course. I have nothing to hide."

Charli smiled. They'd just see about that.

"For the record, Mami Watu has given permission for my partner, Matthew Church, to record our conversation." She then stated the date, time, and location to make it official.

If Mami was flustered, she didn't reveal it, the smile still plastered on her face. "What do you need to ask me? Is this about your reading?"

When Charli hesitated at the mention of the reading, Matthew stepped in. "We're not here to discuss anything to do directly with Detective Cross. We'd rather discuss your relationship to Jefferson Brown."

Mami Watu shut her eyes for a moment before taking a step forward. "Why do you assume I have one?"

"Do you?" Charli's even tone oozed calm and collected. Inwardly, she was fuming, but she kept her voice level and her facial expressions curious and friendly.

"Not at all." Mami's smile faltered, her hand fidgeting with a gold and emerald bracelet on her left wrist.

Charli was the first to break eye contact, not wanting to come across as combative. She let her gaze roam around the room, landing on various trinkets, feigning interest in her surroundings rather than in their subject.

"Are you sure? You don't know Jefferson at all?" Matthew pushed his phone closer to the woman.

But the more Charli and Matthew relaxed, the more agitated Mami became.

"Wait, you think *I* did this?" Mami let out a sarcastic chuckle. "You're kidding me, right? I'm not a murderer, Detectives."

"We're not accusing you. We simply want to ask you some questions, and we would appreciate your cooperation."

Matthew attempted a reassuring smile, but it stopped short of his eyes.

But evidently, Mami could see through Matthew's ploy. Gone was Mami's pleasant façade.

Charli took a step toward Mami. "What was your relationship with Dawn Rita Mollette?"

Fury rolled off the woman in waves. "Just what are you trying to accuse me of? I've already told you that our relationship was strictly business. I may have disliked Dawn, but that doesn't mean I killed her."

Charli held up a calming hand. "If I get a warrant to search this place, I won't find any curare or psilocybin mushrooms?"

Mami Watu swallowed hard and lifted her chin. "No, you will not. Get whatever warrant you want."

"That's good to know, but I don't need your permission." Charli crossed her fingers that Mami wouldn't call her bluff. She didn't yet have the evidence to justify a warrant.

"Why don't you just tell us the truth?" Matthew's voice was even. "You hated Dawn because she sold drugs to the residents of Old Burn Road. Killing drug dealers is a hobby of yours, right? You all but told me so."

Mami's eyes flickered between the two detectives. She drew her petite body up to her full stature. "I never said anything like that. It's Tany who kills drug dealers, not me."

Charli gentled her voice even more. "We know there is no Tany. You made her up to keep people off your trail. *You* are Tany."

Mami lifted her chin, her eyes shooting daggers. "I think you need to leave now."

The detectives didn't budge.

The smaller woman strode toward them, her frail arms crossed.

*Was this her idea of intimidation?*

Mami propelled her body forward, ramming Matthew with her shoulder. She was met with an immoveable force, bouncing off the hulk like a ping pong ball. She had apparently underestimated the sheer bulk of this man.

Before Charli could blink, Mami's heels slid on the slick tile, her arms flailing to regain her balance. Charli lunged forward, snagging the feisty woman by her slim waist just before she fell on her ass.

As she eased Mami into a nearby chair, something tumbled from the older woman's pocket.

*What the hell?*

Gingerly, Charli reached for the object, picking the toy up by its jet-black pixie cut.

"Oh my god, Matt." The air rushed out of Charli's lungs as she held the doll up for Matthew to see. "Look."

"Is that…" Matthew moved in to get a better look. "Is that supposed to be you?"

"I don't know. Why don't we ask her?" Charli thrust the doll into Mami's face.

Charli held her breath, waiting for the older woman to answer. This could go one of two ways. Mami would deny everything, or she would crack.

*Which would it be?*

The rage seemed to leak out of the older woman as she pushed the doll away. "I didn't want to hurt you, you know." She appeared to shrink even more with each word. "The doll was made specifically so I wouldn't have to harm you. I only wanted to guide you from my direction."

"Yeah?" Charli glanced into the doll's face. Same hair… eyes. The resemblance to her caused goose bumps to raise on her arms. "Just like you didn't want to harm Jefferson or Dawn?"

Matthew pulled up a chair for his partner and another

one for himself. Charli sat immediately, knowing the importance of being on her level and mirroring her stance.

Mami Watu's shoulders dropped, her confidence apparently shaken, though Charli knew the woman could be lying through her teeth.

"No, I admit that I did want to harm those two." Her dark gaze rose to meet Charli's. "But you aren't like them. You improve Savannah. Dawn and Jefferson were destroying their own people for profit. That needed to end by any means necessary. Do you know the awful things Jefferson did?"

Charli leaned forward, the doll dangling from her fingers. "Why don't you tell us?" Rather than taking Mami to the precinct, she wanted her to continue. They were so close to a confession, Charli could almost feel it rising in Mami's throat.

Mami closed her eyes and raised her face to the heavens, her mouth moving as though in prayer. Charli let the silence linger, giving the woman a moment to gather herself.

"Jefferson sold drugs he knew were laced with fentanyl." *Why did she look so old now?* "He could move more product the more potent it was. It didn't matter to him that people would die. And people did die. And if that wasn't bad enough, he actually wanted to use voodoo to keep himself safe from the consequences."

Matthew frowned. "But Jefferson didn't believe in voodoo. He specifically banned any voodoo practitioners from his bar."

Mami let out a sharp laugh. "He didn't avoid voodoo practitioners because of a lack of belief. If he didn't believe, why avoid voodoo at all? No, he believed in voodoo strongly and feared what Tany would do to him if she could get ahold of him. He came to me because he'd heard we worked together and wanted my help to keep him safe from Carl."

"Because Carl had been sending him death threats?" Charli already knew the answer but needed it to come from Mami for the recording.

"Exactly. He wanted me to make sure Carl couldn't hurt him. Carl wanted vengeance for what Jefferson had done to his son. To see him walk through my doors disgusted me. But I saw an opportunity to punish him for what he did."

Matthew nodded as if every word Mami had just said made perfect sense. "So, you wanted to punish Jefferson for his drug dealings. But why drug Carl?"

Mami raised her hands to her temples, grimacing as she gently massaged in circles. "Carl isn't entirely innocent, either. The reason his son became an addict was because Carl was once an addict too. He played a part in his son's death as well. Guilty people are always the ones who place the most blame on others. So, I had a justification for framing him for Jefferson's death. I gave him just enough curare to disorient him but not kill him. With the death threats he'd been sending Jefferson, I figured it would be easy to leap to him as the killer."

Charli ran her finger over the doll she was still gripping in her hand. If it wasn't so creepy, the effigy would be a beautiful piece of art. Nothing like the cloth dolls found at the cemetery.

She turned the doll to face Mami. "What about this? This and all the other dolls in your shop are extravagant. The ones we found on Jefferson and Carl looked nothing like this."

Mami shrugged and repositioned herself on the chair. "I did lie about never buying dolls wholesale. I needed those dolls to plant on the...victims. I couldn't go using my own dolls or else risk the blame falling back on me. I keep dolls on hand that I didn't make so that people may find them and trust in the power of voodoo."

Charli couldn't believe it, but she kept her rage

simmering below the surface. "So, your usage of voodoo is all a form of manipulation. Even you don't believe it works."

"When did I say that?" Mami wrung her hands in her lap, her agitation growing. "I believe in voodoo completely, but I know how hard it is to convince others. So, yes, I do my best to stoke belief when others resist."

"The same way you researched Madeline to make me believe, right?" Charli couldn't let that go. That anyone would use Madeline as a manipulation against her was abhorrent.

Mami's eyes dropped. "Yes, I will admit I did my research, Detective."

"And Tany Speers was always fake?" Matthew pushed the interrogation back on track.

"Oh, no, Tany was very real." Mami turned to face Charli. "When I told you I used to know Tany but became disgusted with her, I meant it."

"You are Tany." Charli's words were soft, simply stating a fact.

Mami pressed her lips together, bowing her chin low. "Yes, but you must understand…in my younger years, I had a dark heart. I became increasingly more disturbed by the choices I had made. I vowed to find the lighter side of voodoo and gave up my persona as Tany for decades. All my energy went into Mami Watu and the shop she ran. My desire became to do good, and I made that happen."

Matthew's laughter rang out and echoed on the shop walls. "You killed two people. I don't think you found the lighter side of voodoo."

"Light and dark are two sides of the same coin, Detective. The coin is easy to flip. I remained in the light for many years, but yes, I was brought back into the darkness. When I saw the increase in overdoses that fentanyl was causing all over the country, Papa Legba pulled me back into the shadows to make a change."

Charli couldn't care less about Mami's philosophical musings. She may really believe in voodoo, but Charli didn't. And listening to this mumbo jumbo was grating on her thinly stretched nerves.

It didn't matter that Mami Watu believed she had been sent on a noble quest by a voodoo deity. Her beliefs didn't make her any less manipulative and evil. The woman had tortured Dawn into one of the worst deaths Charli had ever seen in a case. Or at least, she had instigated and overseen Dawn's torture and dismantling.

Did this slip of a woman have the strength to carry out the poor victim's slaughter, or had she enlisted the help of another equally demented human? Regardless of Mami's role, how could she act as though she were placed upon some moral high ground?

"Don't judge me, Detective Cross. You and I are one and the same. We both aim to make Savannah a better place. But I don't believe your justice system works. If it did, Jefferson would have been locked up years ago."

Charli turned the doll in her hands over and over. "If you think I'm trying to improve my community, why the hell was a voodoo doll of my likeness in your pocket?"

"I needed to steer you away from me so that your life would be spared. I only used the doll for your own benefit."

Charli didn't buy that or her act of nobility. There was no ultimate goodness in her heart driving her actions. This woman was a hardened, vile criminal.

"And how did a woman of your size—"

Before Charli could get the question out, the bell on the front door rang. A tall man with a slick ebony head entered through the shop door. He said nothing but eyed the detectives before walking over to a nearby shelf.

Mami gasped, her hands coming up to her mouth. They trembled in a way Charli hadn't witnessed coming from the normally calm and controlled woman.

Unease settled around Charli like a cold, wet blanket. "Sir, I'm sorry, but you're going to have to leave." She pushed to her feet. "We're in the middle of a police investigation."

Charli expected the man to apologize and walk out, but he didn't even turn around. He faced the shelf and stood unmoving. *Was he deaf?* Maybe he hadn't heard her request.

After exchanging an uncomfortable glance with her partner, Matthew stood and took a step toward the man. "Sir, you need to exit immed—"

"Shhh!" Mami jumped up from the chair, grabbing Matthew by the arm.

The detective stumbled back. "Do not touch me!"

"Be quiet!" Mami Watu's eyes were saucers. Her chest rose and fell in quick succession.

*Was Mami trying to prevent a client from discovering her heinous crimes?*

Mami had gone to great lengths to make sure that she separated her image far from Tany Speers. Or was this something else?

The way she insisted Matthew keep quiet was too bold, the fear in her eyes too real. Would a woman who would soon be shipped off to prison really put her hands on a cop just to save her reputation? She had to know there was no longer a reputation to save.

The man still didn't turn around. His shoulders were high, raised above his neckline. He stood frozen in time, unmoving even when he drew a breath.

*He was tall. And strong. There was no way Mami had the strength to pin Dawn Rita to the wall, but—*

"Oh, for crying out loud." Matthew strode past Mami and approached the man.

Mami clutched at his wrist, but he escaped her grasp. "No…"

As Charli watched the events unfold before her, time stood still.

*Mami Watu wasn't scared for her reputation.*

*She was afraid of this man.*

*He was a danger.*

Charli's previous thoughts flashed through her mind. There was no way Mami Watu, with her petite stature and frail body, had the strength to pin Dawn to her living room wall. Mami would have needed help.

The man was her help.

Charli should have known that right away, and Matthew was about to pay for that mistake.

"No, Matt, wait!" Charli's voice cracked on the last word.

Matthew whipped his head around as the man turned. He was holding a dagger.

The beast raised the gleaming blade, a wicked smile teasing his lips.

Time slowed to a crawl.

"No!" Charli rushed toward her partner, but she knew she was too far away to help him.

*Was she about to lose the only person she had left in this world who truly understood her?* Matthew wasn't a colleague. He was her best friend in this world. The only person she could tell her deepest thoughts to. Matthew was her family.

Legs propelling her forward, Charli pulled out her gun as the seconds ticked by. Helplessness filled her soul as the dagger began its descent. She was about to lose her dearest friend. *Again.*

Charli aimed her gun, but from where she stood, the man was directly behind Matthew. She couldn't shoot the giant without putting a bullet in her partner.

All those years ago, she'd promised herself she would

never lose another person. It was why she had become a police detective. She trained to have the expertise to overpower anyone or anything that threatened to take a life in front of her.

And yet, because of one lost moment in time, all her training was rendered useless. No amount of expertise could force her across the room to push Matthew out of the way of the knife.

Charli could only stare as the man thrust the dagger into Matthew's body.

## 34

Fire seared through Matthew's forearm.

His body had moved before his brain processed the knife hurtling toward him, and he'd blocked what could have been a lethal blow to his neck.

Not that the slash he'd received had been a minor injury. Crimson leaked into the blue pinstripes of his button-down shirt. Red rain splattered the tile floor. This cut was deep, possibly even to the bone. And if Matthew's life wasn't on the line, it might have slowed him down.

But the threat of death drowned out all else. Not even excruciating pain would distract him. The knife still glowed in the man's hand under the fluorescent lights up above. It would be mere seconds until it came his way again. Matthew caught a glimpse of the hollow eyes that stared down at him. His dead gaze was incongruent with the ear-to-ear grin that dominated his attacker's jaw.

*Bastard.*

Fueled by adrenaline and rage, Matthew launched a tight fist straight into the man's throat, enjoying the sensation of bone and cartilage giving beneath his knuckles.

Matthew had gone for the carotid baroreceptor and vagus nerve, but baldy turtled his neck just in time to lessen the full effect of the blow. The big man hadn't gone down like Matthew hoped, but he was distracted enough by his current lack of air to give Matthew the upper hand for a second.

The instinct to fight ran deep within Matthew, a reaction from his reptilian brain in response to the immediate threat on his life. But instinct flushed away like a rushing waterfall, replaced by logical analysis. He had to grab his gun.

With Matthew's right arm gushing blood, it was his left hand that made the reach for his weapon. But by the time Matthew had the barrel pointed at his assailant, the perp was already out the front door.

"Freeze!" Matthew willed his body forward, but the slick red pool below skewed his footing.

The floor rushed toward him. His left hand caught his fall with a sickening smack. Matthew gaped at the lake of blood that now coated his slacks. *Had he already leaked this much blood?*

Charli rushed his way, but he garnered all his strength to shout, "Charli, grab him!"

Matthew's words didn't need to be stated. Charli never needed to be told when to move into action. She was already out the door before Matthew could get the words out.

Even as the door swung closed, Matthew commanded Siri to put out a call to the precinct for backup. A unit was only five minutes away, but would that be soon enough?

Matthew bit his lip, willing himself to stay coherent. Charli would have to handle the brute on her own now. He shuddered. Matthew himself had been barely able to fend him off.

His partner was capable, though. She had her firearm and wasn't on the verge of passing out. It would be a lie to say

Matthew wasn't tempted to go follow her. But realistically, Matthew was a liability. In his weakened state, the perp could focus his assault on Matthew to distract Charli. No, it was better to stay in place and keep Mami Watu from making a quick exit.

*Shit.*

Where was the woman?

Her presence had faded into the background during all the chaos. Matthew's head was clouded by low blood pressure, and he'd nearly forgotten about her.

Matthew's hand flitted out to find the nearby display table to steady himself. When his fingers grazed the smooth wood, he shifted to turn to the place where she once stood, but only her high heels remained.

Barefoot, Mami crept backward, like a mouse scurrying to a hole in a nearby baseboard. *Did she really think she'd be able to slip out unnoticed?*

Training his gun on Mami, Matthew found her only feet from the door. "You aren't going anywhere. Hands up."

But Mami slid her hands into her pockets in defiance. "Detective, I think we both know you're not going to shoot me."

"Try me. Hands out of your pockets, now. Or I'll shoot."

*One second passed.*

*Two.*

*Three.*

*Four.*

The two faced off, and just before the last of Matthew's energy receded, Mami's shoulders sagged, and she raised her hands above her head. She fixated her gaze on the lake of blood that pooled onto the floor. Her eyes lingered on the gore before rising to meet Matthew's.

The voodoo priestess took a step to the right, exposing an oversized gold-trimmed mirror behind her. Matthew's reflection was shocking. Maybe the mirror was one of the kinds normally found in carnivals. Except, instead of this one distorting his features, it sucked all the color from his skin, leaving a ghost in the middle of the voodoo shop.

Fingers gripped around his gun, still aimed at Mami. The metal began to tremble. Mami Watu smiled with glistening eyes. The hope in their dark depths betrayed her thoughts. There was still a chance she could wait him out. If Matthew fainted, she'd be able to slip away.

That couldn't happen. If Charli was out there doing the real work, the least Matthew could do was stay conscious.

Scarves in decorative Haitian print hung on a wall behind the counter. If he could reach them, Matthew might be able to halt the bleeding. But he couldn't take his gun off Mami. She wouldn't hesitate to make a run for it at the earliest opportunity.

Matthew moved his gun into his other hand without changing its position. Flames licked at his forearm. It took all his effort to grip the weapon. With his uninjured hand, he reached for the scarves. A red and blue silk one fell away from the wall, the tail fluttering in the air. The material wasn't thick, but at least Matthew could apply pressure. He wrapped it around the wound, pulling the ends like a rip cord on a parachute. And this was his parachute if it kept him alert.

"You feeling okay there?" Mami's smile taunted him.

"Fresh as a spring breeze." He gasped out a breath. "I think I could go for a run."

"Yeah? How about a chase?"

Matthew put his other hand on his gun, trapping the grip between both palms. "Don't...you dare."

Mami lifted her shoulders, raising her hands even farther. "It was just a suggestion."

Matthew kept his eyes on her every move, her every

expression. Mami Watu oozed confidence. She was no longer the same person who had confessed to murder. *Was Matthew as bad off as Mami seemed to believe he was?*

Charli had to hurry. A faint blur was closing in on Matthew's vision. He stared at Mami through a tunnel that grew darker by the second.

A weight grew on Matthew's eyelids. This was it. Matthew had no choice but to give in to the growing exhaustion as the world around him grew dark.

*Crash!*

His eyes sprang open as a commotion behind the shop jolted Matthew awake. "Charli!" Cold sweat dripped off Matthew's nose, his fear for his partner keeping him conscious.

That fear grew into a crushing boulder on his chest.

Charli didn't answer.

# 35

Charli squinted against the sunbeams that threatened to blind her. Going from the low light of the shop to the blaring sun was a shock to her pupils. Her hand flew to her face to block the fiery rays. She had to see. She had to find the man who had dug a knife into Matthew's arm.

White-hot fury replaced the relief that had washed over Charli when the knife missed her partner's neck. Heat rose from Charli's chest that forced her into action the second the perpetrator began to flee.

Charli had been right on his tail, getting out the door only seconds after him. Just a few feet behind, her feet pushed against the cement as she readied herself to take him down. But that plan was thwarted by the shimmering knife hurtling toward her face.

She crashed against the concrete, and a searing burn emanated from her scraped knees as she dove out of the way. The flying knife clanked against the brick before falling to the ground.

Charli had been distracted for a moment…and the perp was gone.

An alley between Mami Watu's shop and another brick building lined the opposite side of the street. From there, the alley split in two directions. Charli's head shifted from left to right, but the man wasn't there.

Her hand was on her gun as she crept off the cement steps. Loose gravel crunched under her foot. Charli froze. If she couldn't see the man, maybe she could hear him.

Seconds ticked by. *Silence.* There wasn't so much as an echo. Charli couldn't wait any longer. She had to choose a direction. The alternative was to let him get away without so much as a positive identification.

She swung one foot to the left, darting in that direction of the alley, only pausing when the wall of Mami's shop ended. Between Mami's shop and the next building was a gap. Not big enough to call an alley, but wide enough for the man to squeeze through.

Charli's instinct to stop along the edge was spot-on. *Whoosh.* A rush of air swept by Charli's face, the wicked blade of a second knife a fraction of an inch away from grazing her cheek.

*How many knives did the bastard have?*

He missed once, but now that he'd exposed his position, she knew he wouldn't let up. Out of instinct, Charli moved backward as he moved forward, swiping once more.

Gun in hand, Charli smashed into his wrist. The knife clattered to the gravel, the metal sliding against the rocks to a screeching halt.

The man stopped to study the knife, and she could tell that he was considering whether he could make a reach for it. It was that split second of time Charli needed.

She rushed him, sweeping her leg under his.

The brute fell hard, his face scraping the brick building as he tumbled to the ground.

Bits of bloody flesh clung to rough brick.

Not waiting a second, Charli grabbed both of his wrists and pinned a knee in his back. Forced to holster her gun so she could cuff him, she could only hope she had enough pressure on his back and enough torque in his shoulders to keep him in place.

"Don't move!" Charli had cuffs in her pocket, ready to detain him.

As he wriggled under Charli's grip, his shoulder knocked against a tower of cardboard boxes. They were haphazardly stacked, like a game of Jenga coming to its end. That small movement was enough to send them toppling down.

The top box fell open, releasing a pile of voodoo dolls onto the ground. The eyes of one specific doll penetrated Charli's soul. That face was so familiar. In ten years, she hadn't forgotten it.

*Madeline.*

The wind rushed from Charli's lungs. The sudden tachycardia in Charli's chest caused her muscles to relax ever so slightly as she tried to pull herself together.

In that moment of distraction, the man bucked Charli off his back. She scurried to get to her feet, but he lunged at her, his full weight ramming into Charli's torso, pushing her into the gravel. Her gun flew from her hand and clattered to the ground several feet away.

Refusing to give up, Charli stuck out her foot. In one swift motion, she clipped the man in the back of his knees, and he came crashing down with her, bashing his head against the pavement when he fell.

Charli shuffled to her feet. "Don't move!"

This man would not get away. Not after the way he'd gone for Matthew's throat. He was a hardened killer and must be stopped.

Still stunned from his head injury, the man lay sprawled on the ground.

Grabbing her gun, Charli inched toward him. "Put your hands on your head."

After several seconds, he did what she said. Knee in his back again, she slapped one cuff on his wrist before yanking his other arm down to do the same.

Knives. She needed to make sure he didn't have more blades on his person.

"Do you have anything else sharp on you? I'm going to be pissed if I get so much as a papercut."

His head turned, though he remained unresponsive. Blood flowed down the side of his head.

"Who are you?" Charli shouted into his ear.

The man wouldn't respond. Not to that question or any of the others Charli yelled out to him. He didn't whimper from the pain, either.

It wasn't long before officers arrived.

"Detective Cross?" Feet shuffled against concrete.

"I'm back here!"

As soon as they got close enough, Charli started spewing questions. "How's Matthew? Did you get Mami Watu?" Heavy breath punctuated Charli's words.

"Another officer is taking her to his car. And we've got an ambulance on the way for Detective Church."

*Matthew.*

As soon as the officers had the assailant in their grasp, Charli ran into the shop. Her partner was collapsed onto the floor next to the counter, another officer kneeling beside him. A thin scarf fell loosely from his bleeding forearm.

Charli grabbed her jacket and used that to stave off the bleeding instead. Matthew's face was a deathly pale, like he'd been dashed in a glass of milk.

But he'd be fine. Charli had to remind herself of that.

He'd lost color from the bleeding, but she knew this amount of blood was not enough to kill someone. As long as he got medical attention soon, he would be okay. That was all that mattered.

That and punishing the monsters who'd done this to him.

# 36

The interrogation room held a haunting emptiness. It had been so long since Charli had been in here without Matthew. Sure, sometimes Matthew stepped out briefly, but he was always here at the precinct with her.

If he'd been on vacation or home sick, maybe the space wouldn't ring so hollow. Charli's heart sank, knowing that he was suffering in the emergency room alone. Matthew had no family or friends outside of the precinct who could be with him. If it were any other time, Charli would be by his side.

But one of them had to handle Mami Watu and the psychopath who had attacked him. There was no time to waste. Charli needed to confront Mami while everything was still fresh.

Through the glass, Mami's eyes were trained on the wall in front of her. Not a second went by when this woman didn't appear to be calculating her next move. Charli couldn't allow her more time to think. Sometimes, it helped to allow a perp to sweat it out. But Mami was unshaken. Her petite frame was an unmoving statue.

Charli could be a rock too, though. She pulled the door

open at a snail's pace, expressing no sense of urgency. When she reached her chair, she pulled it out from the table in the same painstaking manner. Mami's head traced the chair legs' motion across the floor, and she watched Charli closely as she started the video recording.

"I'm sorry about your partner. Will he be all right?" Mami's hands folded in her lap, fingers intertwined.

"Do you want him to be all right?" Charli's words were not accusatory.

Although rage boiled within her veins, Charli would suffer it in silence. She would not get aggressive, not yet. It was better to keep Mami calm by showing genuine interest in her motives.

Occasionally, a calm demeanor matched with feigning empathy was enough to get a criminal to admit to their crimes. As calculated as Mami was, there was a moment back in her shop when she had genuinely tried to stop Matthew from approaching the man who slashed him. She undoubtedly was aware of what this monster was capable of.

*Had she actually wanted to keep Matthew out of harm's way?*

"I do. You know, I was honest when I spoke to you earlier, Detective. I didn't want to involve you. And I engaged in many spells to try to steer you away. I think you're like me. You want to see justice in this community. I simply didn't want you to prevent me from carrying out my own justice."

Charli could hardly see cold-blooded murder as justice. How could cutting up Dawn while she was still alert be anything close to fair? That was an agony that nobody deserved.

"And what does justice mean for you?" Charli's words were as cool as a mountain breeze and equally as airy.

"It means punishing those that cause endless suffering. Jefferson has been poisoning our streets for a decade. Children no older than sixteen were dying from fentanyl and other drug overdoses. You've been out on Old Burn, Detective, so you have seen what I've seen. There are teenagers hooked on these drugs and left to fend for themselves. They spend their nights homeless, cold, soothing aching bellies with a glass pipe."

"And you believed Dawn Rita was responsible for this?"

Mami's eyebrows moved closer to her hairline. "Of course she was. She was selling out on Old Burn. And even if the people out there believe she's helping them, they're dying in the long run. Besides, Dawn was also one of the few people who knew Tany wasn't real. I didn't need her stopping me by going to the police."

Charli leaned back in her chair. She wasn't expecting Mami to be so forthcoming.

"You're telling me the truth here, aren't you?"

Mami released a heavy breath of relief. "I know when the jig is up. I'm caught red-handed. And if I am sitting here in your precinct right now, it is because the spirits willed it. They want me to cease what I'm doing, so I will."

It was possible Mami actually believed she was doing good work for her community. She didn't strike Charli as the kind of murderer who killed for her own pleasure. That explained why Jefferson's death had appeared so peaceful.

Charli couldn't forget Dawn's passing, though.

"I want to believe that you thought you were doing the right thing, that you didn't want to kill people. But then I remember how Dawn died. It seems unnecessarily brutal if all you wanted to do was prevent addiction from spreading on Old Burn Road."

Mami's face contorted. Her lips dropped, and her head shook slowly. "I didn't want that. It wasn't what I had planned. But I couldn't stop him. Admittedly, I was the one who asked for his protection. I am responsible for my association with him."

"Who is 'he'?"

Their attacker didn't have a wallet or any other identification. The man now sat in a hospital room, refusing to speak.

"I don't know his real name. He only went by the name 'D.' We first met on my hunt for curare, but he figured out what I'd done after Jefferson's death. D didn't care for Jefferson, either, and he said he appreciated the work I was doing. When the cops became involved, he said he'd protect me. But I didn't know what that truly meant. I never wanted it to get this out of hand."

Charli found it hard to believe D was on board with Mami Watu offing drug dealers. Clearly, he was a dealer himself. More likely, this was a manipulation of Mami to ensure he was safe from her attacks while killing his competition at the same time. But it wasn't necessary for Charli to mention this to Mami. If Charli implied she'd been tricked, Mami may grow defensive.

Mami raised a hand to her throat, her face draining of its color.

Charli leaned forward, her voice filled with concern. "Are you all right?"

Mami gave a slight nod, gingerly lowering her hand. "Yes, I will be fine. Anyway, I would have never tortured Dawn that way. There was a spell I did to help ensure she had a peaceful passing into the afterlife despite her anguish. That death has haunted me every second since it happened. And the spirits know. They're taking pity on me in allowing me to be caught."

It was ridiculous that after everything she'd done, Mami still wholeheartedly believed in voodoo. She used drugs to mimic the effects of her spells, yet she didn't see this as a sham? Again, to say this out loud would be to shut out Mami.

Charli kept her mouth shut.

"Initially, you weren't planning to confess, right? You wanted to frame Carl Perkins for this."

Mami Watu bit her bottom lip. "I believed I was going to continue to do my work for months and years to come. Healing this world was what got me started in voodoo, in fact. The only reason Tany ever existed was because I was willing to dabble in the dark side of voodoo. A part of me wanted to believe I still had the piss and vinegar I did at twenty-five. But the truth is, I quit dark magic for a reason. I don't have the heart for it. I'm...tired."

Charli studied Mami's face, the smooth skin barely wrinkled. But her face was gaunt, her eyes tired. *Ancient* would have been a better word.

This entire mess made little sense to Charli. "So why do it at all? If you were done with black magic, why start again?"

Darkness filled Mami's eyes. "I got some news from my doctor that changed my perspective. I felt hopeless about my life. How long I lived without purpose, so I found some."

*Was Mami terminally ill?*

"What news was that?"

"It doesn't matter now, Detective. And I won't be sharing in a ploy to gain any sympathy. I'm not looking for any. I only hope when Papa Legba welcomes me into the underworld, he understands my intentions were always good."

"So, just to be clear, you're saying you had no idea Dawn was going to die that way?" It was important Charli get exact clarification on this.

"I knew she was to be pinned to the wall. It was part of our plan to frame Carl, in fact. Nobody would believe a woman of my age and stature could chop a woman into pieces and nail her to the wall, especially not a woman with my medical condition. It was meant to look as though a strong man had committed the act. But Dawn was supposed to be dead when D dismantled her body."

Charli's mouth opened to reply, but a knock on the door made her pause. Charli's head whipped to the door. Her mind instantly went to Matthew, though she knew he couldn't possibly be here.

"Excuse me for a moment." Charli left Mami, still sitting with folded hands.

On the other side of the interrogation room door, Ruth stood with a file in hand.

"We've got an ID on the man who stabbed Matthew. His name is Del Adamson. We had his prints in the system. He's got three warrants out for his arrest in three different Georgia cities."

Charli took the file from her. "According to Mami, he was the one who killed and dismembered Dawn Rita."

Ruth raised an eyebrow. "You believe her?"

"I do, actually." Mami was right about one thing. She didn't seem capable of physically committing that murder. "She didn't announce it to feign innocence. In fact, she openly admits she planned to kill Dawn Rita and played an equal part in her death."

"And why would Del agree to do this with Mami?"

"I think it was probably an easy way for him to eliminate his competition."

Ruth stepped around Charli to look through the observation window at Mami, who still hadn't moved. "Well, hopefully, you can find out. Del says he'll talk, but only to you."

That was a surprise. "Only to me?"

"That's what he says. He's restrained, so even if he has something planned, it would be impossible for him to execute it. If you've got enough to arrest Mami, wrap this up and head to the hospital."

"Sure. I'm nearly finished with her." There was just one more thing Charli had to know, for her own benefit.

The recording device was still running when Charli took

her seat again, and she was tempted to turn it off but didn't. For a moment, she allowed a wave of silence to crash between them.

The seconds passed, and the tension grew to be too much for Mami. "Is there something you would like to say, Detective?"

"How did you know about Madeline?" Charli could not let this go.

By now, she was able to easily shrug off voodoo magic as a falsehood. Almost everything in the case that approached the paranormal world had been explained, except this. Charli needed this last bit of information.

"I paid D to dig up information on both you and your partner. He was able to find that Detective Church was divorced. In your case, the public library had an old copy of your yearbook that contained a memorial page for Madeline. You were plastered all over it."

Charli wasn't even aware the library kept old yearbook copies. "So, you sought information to rattle us?"

"It was an old tool Tany used. I liked to have the mental edge. In this case, though, I fear using that information was exactly what led you to me." Mami Watu tilted her head forward. "Am I right?"

Charli saw no reason not to admit this. "If you hadn't tried to taunt me with Madeline's name, yes, I probably would have continued to investigate Carl instead. That did set me off."

Mami's chest rose and fell like a deflating balloon. "That choice led me to this moment. But this moment is exactly where I'm supposed to be. I will not wallow in my regrets."

The way she spoke, she still resembled the wise, professional businesswoman Charli had met on the first day of the investigation. It was easy to forget how she had ended two lives and attempted to frame someone else for the crime.

At her core, though, this woman was a killer. Her intentions made no difference. Charli shared her passion for getting criminals off the street of Savannah, but *she'd* never been tempted to end someone's life. In a civilized society, there were better ways to attain justice.

Charli cleared her throat. "Mami Watu, we're placing you under arrest for the murder of Jefferson Brown and an accessory to the murder of Dawn Rita Molette."

Mami Watu inclined her regal head, her dark gaze intent on Charli. "I expected nothing less."

## 37

A symphony of beeping machines filled the emergency room's hallway. It took Charli back to memories of sleeping in her mother's room, lulled to sleep by the sounds of her monitor. The noise didn't bother Charli one bit. The absence of the beeps was what Charli had feared most, as it meant her mother's inevitable passing had come.

But she pushed the thoughts of her mom aside. She was here for two things: to interrogate Del Adamson and check in on Matthew.

Matthew would come first. Del Adamson probably should have been Charli's priority, but she couldn't focus on that without assuring herself Matthew would be okay. She knew he would be. It was only a deep cut, after all. But seeing him bleeding out on the floor of Mami's shop had disturbed Charli deeply. She'd work better when she saw him back to his old self.

The triage nurse had told her to check in on room 106. The metal door was propped wide open when she arrived. Even so, she knocked against the frame.

"You ready for visitors?" Charli averted her eyes to the

top of the wall so she couldn't look inside the room. It would give Matthew time to get decent if he wasn't already.

"Ready as I'll ever be."

Her fear dissipated into the air around her the second she heard his voice. He was joking around. That was a good sign.

Upon turning the corner, a bit of that fear returned to create a lump in her chest. Matthew may have been talking, but he was still as pale as a ghost.

"Are you all right?" Charli pulled a chair close to his bed.

"I'll be fine. Doc said I lost a fair amount of blood, so I'm not feeling great. But I'll be back to normal soon."

"Well, I heard most of the force has already been by to donate blood. Apparently, Janice was first in line. Hope you're ready for that woman to be coursing through your veins."

Matthew let out a breathy laugh. "You'd love that, huh?"

The bandage on Matthew's forearm was reminiscent of the white marble floor that collected his blood. It, too, was tinged with red, a stark contrast to the edges of the clean bandage.

Matthew followed Charli's gaze. "Twenty-four stitches is what it took, apparently. But I'll be fine as soon as they get my blood pressure back up."

"Does it hurt?"

"It did. But whatever they gave me, that's the real magic in this world. Forget voodoo. Just hook me up to an IV."

Charli chuckled. "Glad you're feeling better. I gotta say, it was scary to see you like that."

Matthew stared directly at Charli, pausing for a moment before speaking again. "In all honesty, it was the scariest thing I've ever experienced on the job. I'd never fainted before. It feels like death."

Charli held his gaze. There was a deep, innate connection

between the two of them. It provided a warmth Charli hadn't felt since before Madeline passed.

For years, Charli had heard stories of the impenetrable bond between two partners. Charli had been close to Matthew for a long time, but she'd never felt a connection quite like this. It was almost telepathic, like she could embody what he was feeling. His emotions forced their way into her veins and then became her own.

Theirs wasn't unlike the relationship she'd shared with Madeline. Being friends since they were toddlers, Madeline could read Charli's mind. And Charli assumed she'd never be able to share that with anyone else.

Though she never engaged in physical touch voluntarily, Charli found herself reaching out to Matthew's hand. "I'm so glad you're okay. I don't know what I'd do without you."

"I do. You'd lose Mami Watu. She's in custody, right?"

"Oh yeah, and she's admitting to everything she's done. I think she's actually relieved to have been caught."

"And the guy who slashed me?"

"His name is Del Adamson. He's a drug dealer with multiple warrants out for his arrest. He has a concussion and is recovering here too. Apparently, he's awake now and wants to speak with me alone."

A gleam formed in Matthew's eye that Charli had only seen from her father. It was protective, with a hint of concern. "You shouldn't see him alone."

"It'll be fine. He's restrained. And if he's willing to talk, I want to listen. Don't worry about me." She flexed her muscles and bobbed her eyebrows. "Worry about him."

Matthew glanced from side to side as he tried to figure that one out. "Why would I worry about him?"

"Because I want to strangle that asshole for what he did to you."

A hint of a smile formed on Matthew's lips. "Don't go doing anything crazy, Charli."

"I'll contain myself. Don't worry. I'd better head over there now. Want me to stop by again before I leave?"

Matthew shook his head. "Don't worry about it, really. I know you've got a lot to do on this case now that I'm in here. I'll call you when they say I can go home."

"Do that." She patted his shoulder, resisting the urge to lean down and hug him for a hundred years. "I'll come pick you up."

Del's room was only three doors down from Matthew's. Despite Del being restrained, this didn't sit right with Charli. She wanted that man as far away from Matthew as humanly possible. Hopefully, they would let Matthew go home soon.

Finding Del's room wasn't difficult, considering the officer posted outside his door. Del's hands were cuffed to the rails of his bed. He wore a loose hospital gown, a large bandage wrapped around his head where he had bashed it on the concrete. From the doorway, Charli could only glimpse the back of his head. He was facing the window, not moving an inch. Even when Charli spoke, he did not turn to face her.

"I hear you wanted to talk to me." Charli moved around the bed, standing next to the window so that Del was now forced to make eye contact with her.

The grin that filled his cheeks sent a shiver down Charli's spine. There was no emotion in his eyes, even when he smiled. Charli waited for words to fill the empty room, but he said nothing.

That was fine. Charli had a good idea of what they could talk about. She pulled his file up on her phone before turning her recorder on. After getting his approval to record their conversation, she stated the time, date, and other particulars before getting down to business.

"Looks like you're wanted on drug charges in three different cities. You were on trial for murder in New Orleans only four years ago. And you've been convicted of a B and E on a Catholic church that you defaced. That's quite the rap sheet."

Del shrugged. "It could be longer."

Del and Mami, despite both being criminals, appeared to be opposites. Mami expressed regret at having committed crimes she believed were for the greater good. But Del was downright proud of his actions.

That was fine by Charli, though. If he was prideful of his criminal activity, perhaps he could be coaxed to brag about it.

"What brought you to Mami Watu?" Charli pretended to continue reading his file.

"I stop by her shop often. Whenever I need materials for my spells."

That was a surprise. "You practice voodoo?"

Charli was aware Del stopped by Mami's shop, but not that he was a practitioner himself.

"You think Dawn and Mami are the only ones? I was practicing in New Orleans with the big shots while they've been twiddling their thumbs down here in Savannah."

"New Orleans is the real voodoo scene, huh? Then why did you leave?"

For the first time, the smile faded from Del's face. "I ran into some Haitians that were using voodoo for seriously sick shit—trafficking children, possessing innocent bystanders to commit their crimes. I'm no saint, Detective, but even I have my standards. And I heard Mami Watu does too. I came to Savannah to seek her out."

"Okay, so you hear of Mami and her shop. You come to meet her. And then what?"

"I became her curare supplier. Didn't know what she was up to at first, but I wasn't about to be part of anyone else's evildoing, so I looked into it. I heard about Jefferson on the news and figured things out. Told her I was on her side. I wanted to use voodoo to make the world a better place too."

Charli repressed the desire to scoff. "But you're a drug dealer yourself."

Del's lips curled. "But not that fentanyl shit! I wasn't killing anyone with my drugs. I was just giving people what they wanted."

With Del already growing defensive, Charli backed off to keep him talking. "Mami Watu said you were the one who maimed Dawn Rita in her last moments." She fully expected Del to deny this.

"Maybe I did. Maybe I didn't. Maybe I can tell you if we make a deal."

Charli narrowed her eyes, trying to imagine what he was thinking. This was an open-and-shut case. She couldn't fathom what he'd bring to the table. Mami Watu had already confessed her guilt.

"What kind of deal?"

"Before coming to Savannah, I knew of several voodoo gangs taking part in some pretty nasty crimes. Surely you wanna stop human trafficking."

"The state might be interested in that, yeah. I can't make you any promises myself, but I can get you in touch with people who can." Charli was careful to leave this open-ended. She kept her fingers crossed, hoping Del didn't hold out for a written agreement from the D.A. before he confessed. "Now, did you murder Dawn Rita?"

He settled back into his pillow. "I'll answer that once I've talked to the D.A."

*Crap.*

"Not going to tell me why?"

Del closed his eyes, and his lips turned upward into his

cheeks once again. He let the room fill with silence as he kept his thoughts to himself.

It didn't much matter, though. They had a pretty solid case against him so far, and if he was going to maintain his silence, Charli could always question him later. Maybe a few days in jail would soften him to conversation.

"I suppose we'll talk further down at the station." The sun warmed Charli's cheek as she strolled past the window, giving time for Del to respond.

"You saw something, didn't you?" By the time Del opened his mouth, Charli was nearly at the doorway.

She turned to him. He was still facing the window. "Saw what?"

"Something was in that box of dolls. I saw your face. You were horrified. What did you see?"

All the air seemed to leave the room. "Is this why you wanted to see me?" Charli shuddered, hoping Del couldn't read her mind. Surely he didn't know she had seen Madeline's face on one of the dolls.

"Actually, yes. It's nice to be reminded that I can see these things in people. It's why I got into voodoo in the first place." He turned to face her, his dark eyes meeting hers directly. "And I see a darkness in you."

Charli shook her head and took a couple of steps into the hall. She didn't have to entertain this. She had a case to wrap up, paperwork to finish, a D.A. to speak to.

But on her third step, something kept Charli's foot frozen in place. A series of memories flashed before her like clips in a movie trailer. *How the doll had looked so much like Madeline. Dawn Rita telling her she'd been marked.*

Slowly, almost without her mind's instruction, Charli walked back into Del's room.

"This darkness that you see in me…what does it look like?"

Those dark eyes examined her for an uncomfortably long moment. "Tendrils. A bunch of black tendrils that wrap themselves around you. I think nonbelievers refer to it as 'obsession.'"

Charli turned on her heel and stalked from the room. This was ridiculous. She was giving Del more attention than he deserved.

She had a case to finish.

# 38

Charli had every intention of driving back to the precinct, but Del's words were bouncing around her head like a rogue ping-pong ball.

Voodoo wasn't real. Charli knew that. But what she'd seen on that doll was so vivid.

There was only one way she'd be able to push this out of her head. She had to return to Mami Watu's shop.

Forensics was still there when Charli arrived, analyzing the crime scene. She didn't step inside, though, but only glanced in the window as she walked toward the alley where she'd chased Del.

What Charli wanted was not inside Mami's shop but outside of it. Charli snapped her eyes shut and paused. A magnetic pull of emotions had split her attention.

*What was she doing here? What was she expecting to find? Did she want to look at that box of voodoo dolls and find Madeline's face?*

That would be disturbing, absolutely. But it would mean she wasn't crazy. That what she'd seen was real.

But what if she found nothing? What did that mean?

Charli didn't want to analyze it any longer. Her eyes snapped open to the world around her. She moved to the box of voodoo dolls that had been flipped over. Pulling a pair of gloves from her pocket, she snapped them on. Taking a deep breath, she grabbed the box and lifted it off the pile of dolls and...

*Nothing.* There was nothing. All these straw dolls were identical. None of them looked like Madeline's face.

Then why had she seen it? Why had Madeline's dark eyes stared into her soul? Was she marked as Dawn had said? Had obsession overtaken Charli's life like Del implied?

Metal clanked against the brick wall as someone opened a gate at the other end of the alley. Charli whipped around.

"Detective Cross, I was told you'd arrived." Officer Lancaster held the gate open for Charli to walk through.

She'd been in such a hurry to get out back, she hadn't noticed that Vice was already on scene.

"Officer Lancaster, I'm glad you're working this case." It was the truth. Charli trusted Lancaster's work. And after the insanity that had unraveled in this case, she wanted someone competent on board.

"I thought you'd like to know what we've found so far."

"I would, yes." Charli moved up the steps, peeled off the disposable gloves, and took the new ones and booties he held out. She slipped them on and followed him into the shop.

"Up in the apartment, we found two different drugs in large quantities. There was a plastic bag full of curare. And in several glass jars were dried caps of magic blue gym."

"Magic blue gym?" *What the hell was that?*

"They're a type of mushroom, psychedelic in nature."

"Let me guess, they contain psilocybin." Charli remembered Soames's report on Dawn Rita's body.

"You got it. Only two drugs we've been able to find so far, but we're still searching."

Charli doubted they'd find anything more. Mami had made her disdain for illicit drugs clear. She was willing to kill drug dealers. Unless she was lying about her motives, there was no way she'd harbor narcotics herself.

"Thank you, Officer. I appreciate the hard work of your team."

Truth be told, Charli wasn't much interested in that right now. She'd expected both drugs to be found in Mami's possession. It was only a matter of time.

What she hadn't expected was to see Madeline's face plastered on a voodoo doll.

Charli pulled her gloves and booties off once she was outside, placing them in a plastic baggie for the forensics team. Heat blazed against her exposed skin as she signed out of the logbook. The brief moment in the sun had her rushing to the car to flip on the AC. She didn't make a move to drive off, though.

Instead, Charli let the chilled air blow the short strands of her hair around like a hurricane. The sensation grounded her when she needed it most. A few deep breaths of the icy breeze calmed her nerves.

This was silly. Voodoo wasn't real. Mami Watu had never read her fortune. She'd admitted it herself. Likewise, if Del had seen obsession in Charli's aura, it wasn't because she practiced voodoo.

It was because she was so obsessed that anyone could see it. Now was as good a time as ever to admit this to herself. She saw Madeline's face because it rarely left her mind. And Charli used her work to avoid the memories.

Maybe Matthew was right. Perhaps Charli needed a vacation. She couldn't run from her past forever. If she continued to try, it wouldn't just be Del who saw darkness surrounding her.

And hadn't this case been the perfect example of where

obsession could lead when it was allowed to take over? Mami Watu was obsessed with clearing the streets of dangerous criminals. So much so, she became one.

It had taken Charli almost a decade to see this issue, but it was time she started taking care of herself. She vowed to figure out how to do that…

Just as soon as she wrapped up this case.

# 39

Photos of crystal-clear ocean waves hitting white sand beaches flipped through Charli's desktop screen. Was the ocean actually that turquoise, or was that photoshopped? She wasn't sure, but she was eager to find out.

It was the only time in her adult life Charli had looked up hotel packages. Torn between Cancun and the Bahamas, Charli kept flipping tabs on her browser. If she could get the time off request approved, perhaps she could be out of the country by mid-October.

Knuckles rapping against wood forced Charli's attention from her computer to the doorway. Matthew's checkered short-sleeve shirt exposed the train track of stitches that traveled up his arm.

"Frankenstein, no!" Charli threw her arms up to hide the smile on her face. "Please, spare me!"

Matthew's nose scrunched up with displeasure. "Hardy-har. You better be nice to me. They say this thing might scar!"

"Oh, please. You look nothing like Frankenstein. You back so soon?"

Only a week had passed since Matthew had been injured. The mama bear in her wanted to send him straight home with a can of chicken noodle soup.

"Just on scut work. Ruth has me answering phones for the rest of the damn week."

Charli feigned excitement. "So, what I'm hearing is I've got a secretary for the next few days?"

"You're pushing it. You really are." As Matthew walked by, he gave her chair a jerky spin.

All teasing aside, it was a relief to have Matthew back. Between Matthew being gone for the week, and his weekend getaway to California during their last case, Charli had been all too lonely.

Well, except for the night spent with Powell. Though that wasn't much fun, and she hadn't told Matthew about it. That night might be best put into the vault.

"So, any details on that deal Del was trying to work out?" Matthew sat down at his desk.

"Apparently, he's got information that the prosecution wants. They're taking the death penalty off the table and will get him into witness protection."

It was a common misconception that witness protection was only for innocent witnesses to reside in safe houses. Witness protection existed in high-security prisons, as well. There were gang members within the prison gates who would be eager to go after Del for the information on human trafficking he provided. Authorities would give him a new name in prison to ensure he wasn't easily discovered.

But it was unlikely either he or Mami Watu would ever see the light of day again. This was good news for Carl Perkins, who was healing well from his curare incident. He was relieved that he no longer had to worry about being a suspect or unexpectedly drugged again.

And Charli was glad to provide that relief. After what he

went through with his son, Carl deserved a bit of peace. Charli didn't share Mami's opinion that Carl deserved what he had coming because of his past drug use.

Charli believed that people were redeemable. They could grow, could become better individuals who contributed to society. Charli wouldn't be part of the justice system if she didn't believe that.

Of course, there were crimes that were irredeemable, and that included murder. The rates of recidivism for homicide were too high to expect any murderer to change their ways.

Though, there was a chance that Mami Watu's crimes were specific to her recent diagnosis. Evidently, she had inoperable stage four glioblastoma. The brain tumor was pressed against the prefrontal cortex, the part of the brain responsible for decision-making. It could explain why Mami had begun acting so impulsively after decades of good behavior.

Charli had wondered if Mami Watu's lawyer planned to use this defense at her trial—not that she'd live long enough to see a courtroom—but she'd gotten word yesterday that the woman had pled guilty. That didn't surprise Charli. Mami hadn't seemed too bothered about being sent off to prison.

Matthew sighed as he picked up his phone and slammed it back down on the receiver. "Better get used to that motion. I'm going to be doing it a lot over the next few days."

"Don't worry about all the menial work Ruth has you doing. It's not like we have a case right now, anyway." Charli attempted to console him.

"Actually, you just got one."

Ruth's voice caused both Charli and Matthew to flinch. That woman moved like a cat sometimes. She could slide into a space like a predator on the hunt, without the ground shifting noisily under her feet.

"We do?" Charli swiveled in her chair toward her.

"You do. And it's a weird one."

"You're kidding, right?" Matthew scoffed. "I mean, how can it be weirder than zombies and voodoo dolls?"

Ruth tilted her head. A crease formed between her eyebrows, the way it always did when she scowled. "Someone stole a body from the local mortuary."

"I stand corrected," Matthew murmured.

"Wait, why would someone even do that?" The image of someone attempting to transport a cold, hard body set in rigor mortis away from the place it was supposed to go was absurd.

Ruth stood up straight. "I don't know. It's your job to figure that out. So, go do your job. The mortician is waiting to speak to you."

"Wait, can I go too?" Matthew flashed Ruth pleading eyes.

"Yes, yes. You both can go. Just try to avoid any incoming knives, please, Detective Church."

"I'll do my best."

Just as silently as she came, Ruth disappeared, leaving Charli and Matthew to glance at each other.

"Ready for another whirlwind?" Matthew flashed his partner a crooked smile.

Charli's gaze drifted one last time to the glistening sand that lit up on her computer screen. For the first time in a long time, she'd actually been excited about getting away from her job.

But if there was a case she had to attend to, her inner peace would have to wait. She clicked off the screen.

"Ready when you are."

*The End*

*To be continued...*

Thank you for reading.

All of the *Charli Cross Series* books can be found on Amazon.

## ACKNOWLEDGMENTS

How does one properly thank everyone involved in taking a dream and making it a reality? Here goes.

In addition to our families, whose unending support provided the foundation for us to find the time and energy to put these thoughts on paper, we want to thank the editors who polished our words and made them shine.

Many thanks to our publisher for risking taking on two newbies and giving us the confidence to become bona fide authors.

More than anyone, we want to thank you, our readers, for clicking on a couple of nobodies and sharing your most important asset, your time, with this book. We hope with all our hearts we made it worthwhile.

Much love,

*Mary & Donna*

# ABOUT THE AUTHOR

**Mary Stone**

Mary Stone lives among the majestic Blue Ridge Mountains of East Tennessee with her two dogs, four cats, a couple of energetic boys, and a very patient husband.

As a young girl, she would go to bed every night, wondering what type of creature might be lurking underneath. It wasn't until she was older that she learned that the creatures she needed to most fear were human.

Today, she creates vivid stories with courageous, strong heroines and dastardly villains. She invites you to enter her world of serial killers, FBI agents but never damsels in distress. Her female characters can handle themselves, going toe-to-toe with any male character, protagonist or antagonist.

Discover more about Mary Stone on her website.
www.authormarystone.com

**Donna Berdel**

Raised as an Army brat, Donna has lived all over the world, but no place has given her as much peace as the home she lives in with her husband near Myrtle Beach. But while she now keeps her feet planted firmly in the sand, her mind goes back to those cities and the people she met and said goodbye to so many times.

With her two adopted cats fighting for lap space, she brings those she loved (and those she didn't) back as characters in her books. And yes, it's kind of fun to kill off anyone who was mean to her in the past. Mean clerk at the grocery store...beware!

Connect with Mary Online

facebook.com/authormarystone
goodreads.com/AuthorMaryStone
bookbub.com/profile/3378576590
pinterest.com/MaryStoneAuthor

Made in United States
North Haven, CT
02 July 2022

20899553R00137